Julia Gillian

(and the Art of Knowing)

by Alison McGhee

with pictures by
Drazen Kozjan

SCHOLASTIC PRESS NEW YORK

LIBRARY OF CONGRESS CATALOGING-IN-PUBLICATION DATA
McGhee, Alison, 1960–
Julia Gillian (and the Art of Knowing) / by Alison McGhee;
illustrated by Drazen Kozjan. — 1st ed. p. cm.

Summary: Nine-year-old Julia Gillian learns a lot about facing fear as she and her St. Bernard, Bigfoot, take long walks through their Minneapolis neighborhood one hot summer, and she seeks the courage to finish a book that could have an unhappy ending.

ISBN-13: 978-0-545-03348-0
ISBN-10: 0-545-03348-9

[1. Fear—Fiction. 2. Saint Bernard dog—Fiction. 3. Dogs—Fiction. 4. Family life—Minnesota—Minneapolis—Fiction. 5. Neighborhood—Fiction. 6. Minneapolis (Minn.)—Fiction.] I. Kozjan, Drazen, ill. II. Title. PZ7 M4784675Jul 2008 [Fic]—dc22 2007024898

10 9 8 7 6 5 4 3 2 08 09 10 11

Printed in the U.S.A. 23
First edition, May 2008

TO ELLEN HARRIS SWIGGETT

—A.M.

FOR MOM

—D.K.

ACKNOWLEDGMENTS

Heartfelt thanks to all who helped make Julia Gillian a reality, especially Kara LaReau, whose insight and enthusiasm made the editing process a joy, Drazen Kozjan, artist extraordinaire, and Marijka Kostiw, book designer. Love and thanks to Brad Zellar for his generous help on this and other books, and to my children, who bring me joy.

CHAPTER ONE

The Art of Knowing

Julia Gillian, her parents, and her dog, Bigfoot, all lived together in a third-floor apartment in south Minneapolis. There was much for the Gillian family to be happy about. Julia Gillian had finished fourth grade and she was looking forward to fifth grade at Lake Harriet Elementary School. Julia Gillian's parents, who were both teachers, liked their jobs and loved their daughter, who was their only child. Bigfoot, Julia Gillian's Saint Bernard, was nine years old and a loyal, healthy dog. On Saturday nights, all the Gillians liked to go to the Quang Vietnamese Restaurant, which made the best egg rolls in Minneapolis. Occasionally, if it had been an especially good week, Julia Gillian's parents allowed her to order a Quang strawberry bubble tea, which came with an extra-thick straw.

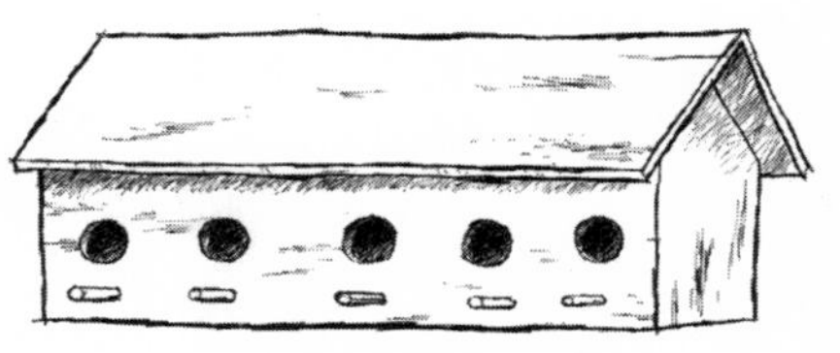

The Gillian family was a talented one. For example, Julia Gillian's mother excelled at making birdhouses out of scraps of wood from Bennett Lumber. Julia Gillian's father was a superb knitter who specialized in fluffy, multicolored winter scarves. And Julia Gillian, at the relatively young age of nine, was good at so many things that they could not be listed on a single side of a piece of lined notebook paper. She now found it necessary to

continue her list of accomplishments on the other side.

Julia Gillian kept her list of accomplishments underneath her mattress. Her mattress was extremely heavy and hard to lift, but in times long past, people kept precious possessions underneath their mattresses, and she considered her list to be a precious possession.

While it couldn't be counted as an accomplishment, Julia Gillian's name was certainly interesting. She was one of those rare people who had a first name for a first name and a first name for a last name, and all her life everyone had called her not just Julia, but Julia Gillian. That was the way it was with some people, such as Julia Gillian, and it made meeting new grownups fun.

Grownup: "Well, hello there. And what might your name be?"

Julia Gillian: "Julia Gillian."

Grownup: "Isn't that a pretty name. And what's your last name?"

Julia Gillian: "Gillian."

This exchange was confusing to the grownup, and it usually took some time before the grownup understood that Julia Gillian's name was not Julia Gillian Gillian. Julia Gillian knew how to be patient, and she was content to wait as the grownup figured it all out.

Grownup: "Let me see if I understand correctly. Your first name is Julia, and your last name is Gillian?"

Julia Gillian: "Indeed it is."

Grownups did not expect a nine-year-old girl to say something like "Indeed it is." But Julia Gillian enjoyed the sound of that particular phrase, and she said it whenever possible. There were many times in life, she had found, when it was possible to use the phrase "Indeed it is" or its equally pleasing cousins "Indeed it was" and "Indeed I do."

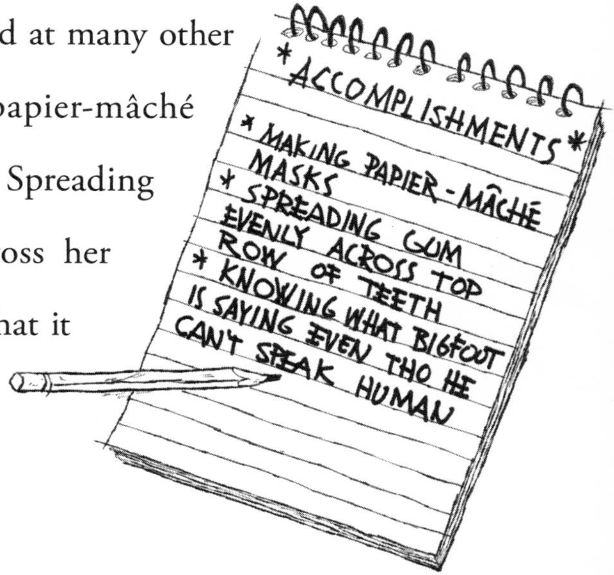

Julia Gillian was good at many other things. Making papier-mâché masks, for example. Spreading her gum evenly across her top row of teeth so that it looked as if she had only one long smooth upper tooth. Knowing what her dog, Bigfoot, was trying to say even though he did not speak in human words.

"I wonder what else I'm good at," Julia Gillian said to Bigfoot.

It was Sunday morning, and she was lying in bed, and Bigfoot was lying on his long magenta pillow next to her bed. There was no telling what else Julia Gillian might be good at, and it was pleasant to think of the possibilities.

"Predictions, maybe," mused Julia Gillian.

She decided to test herself. Julia Gillian could hear her mother down the hall in the kitchen. She was probably finished with her first cup of coffee and ready to make some breakfast.

"Why don't I try to predict Mom's breakfast routine," said Julia Gillian to Bigfoot, "and then we'll go see if I was right."

Bigfoot thumped his tail encouragingly. Julia Gillian closed her eyes and concentrated.

"I bet she's putting two slices of bread in the toaster right at this minute."

She waited a minute.

"Now she's taking them out."

She waited another minute.

"And now she's going to put them on the green seashell plate and spread them with lots of butter."

Julia Gillian had the strong feeling that she was correct, but she wanted verification.

"Come on, Bigfoot," she said. "Let's go see how well we did."

She flung back her sheet and swung both legs out of bed in unison, so that her bare feet touched the floor at the exact same time. The wood floor was slightly sticky, as it always was in the summer heat. Bigfoot rose from his long magenta pillow and, placing both feet before him, performed his customary morning stretch.

At the very moment that they arrived in the kitchen, Julia Gillian's mother lifted a slice of lavishly buttered bread to her mouth and took a bite.

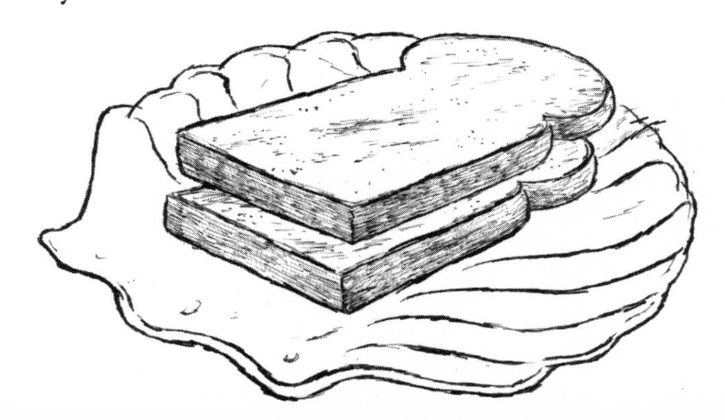

"What are you staring at me for?" said her mother, but not until she had swallowed her bite of toast.

"Because my prediction just came true," said Julia Gillian.

"And what prediction might that be?"

Julia Gillian shook her head. Some things were meant to be secret. Julia Gillian's mother gave her an inquiring look, but she did not attempt to pry the prediction out of her daughter. She was a woman who knew the value of privacy.

"Well, Julia Gillian," said her mother. "I've always said that you were a marvel of a child."

"Thank you."

"In fact, it could be said that you are highly skilled at the art of knowing. I'm sure your father would agree with me."

Julia Gillian liked this. "Skilled at the Art of Knowing" had a nice ring to it. And her mother, as a first-grade teacher, and father, as a high school teacher, certainly were capable of knowing when a child was good at something. Now she could expand the list of things she was good at to include the Art of Knowing.

Julia Gillian's world was in excellent shape.

But the wider world, the world that her excellent world was contained within, seemed to be in extremely poor shape. This much Julia Gillian knew from watching her parents' faces as they read the morning newspaper. She had occasion to observe this phenomenon shortly after adding "skilled at the Art of Knowing" to the list of

things she was good at, while she sat in her chair eating bread and jam, and while her parents sat in their chairs eating their toast and drinking their coffee.

"Can you believe —" her father said, and he pointed to a headline on the front page.

"No, I can't," her mother said.

They looked at each other and shook their heads. Julia Gillian spread more jam on her bread and took a bite. Her parents bent their heads to the paper again. Because it was Sunday, the paper was much larger than usual. Occasionally one of them would grumble, and the other would sigh.

As far as Julia Gillian was concerned, the morning newspaper worried and saddened whoever read it. Here were the words that made her parents most unhappy: *global warming, budget cuts, Middle East,* and anything involving the word *war.*

Her mother sighed.

"Can you believe that here, in the richest country in the world —" she said, and she pointed at another headline.

"I know," said her father. "Terrible, isn't it?"

Was there ever happy news in the newspaper? From her parents' conversation, Julia Gillian guessed not, but she wanted to make sure.

"Father?" said Julia Gillian.

"Daughter?"

When Julia Gillian called her father "Father" that was her signal to him that she was imagining that they lived in a long-ago time, when little girls wore dresses

and tied ribbons in their hair, and parents hid precious possessions under their mattresses, and fathers wore vests and smoked pipes in the parlor, occasionally getting up to stoke the fire. When Julia Gillian's father heard her call him "Father," he always responded by calling her "Daughter." It was part of the routine.

Sometimes, when Julia Gillian and her parents took picnics to the Lake Harriet Rose Garden, they pretended they were a family from long ago. They made cucumber sandwiches and spread their red-and-white-checked tablecloth on the grass and called each other "Daughter" and "Father" and "Mother."

"Is there ever any happy news in the newspaper, Father?"

"Not enough, Daughter. Not nearly enough."

"Then why do you keep reading it, Father?"

"So that I know what is going on in the wider world, Daughter."

This was her father's usual response, and it always confused Julia Gillian. If what was going on in the wider world was that bad, then she was not all that interested in it. She looked at Bigfoot, who was lying under the table with his head resting on top of her left foot, and beamed a thought telepathically to him. *When I grow up I'm not going to read the newspaper.* Bigfoot opened one eye and looked up at her. Then he thumped his tail. Bigfoot and Julia Gillian were skilled at the art of understanding each other, including telepathic beaming. This was one of the many reasons why Bigfoot was the dog of Julia Gillian's dreams.

CHAPTER TWO

The Green Book

Julia Gillian decided to leave her worried parents at the kitchen table with their unhappy, larger-than-usual Sunday newspaper. She herself was not much of a reader. This was a source of dismay to her parents, who, as teachers, believed that reading was fundamental. They often brought home library books that they thought Julia Gillian might like, but after a few pages she would give up. Books in general were not to her liking.

The one book that Julia Gillian had thought she might like was a green one that she had found on her own. It had been sitting in a bin outside Magers & Quinn Booksellers, on Hennepin Avenue. The sign on the bin read ALL BOOKS $1.00. One dollar was an excellent price

Knitting Today
ALL BOOKS $1.00

for a book, and the green book had immediately captured Julia Gillian's attention because there was a picture of a dog on the front cover.

"Dad, can I buy this book?"

"Do you mean *may* you buy that book?" said Julia Gillian's father, who was a stickler for correct grammar.

"*May* I buy this book?"

"Sure you may," her father had replied, thrilled that his child had found a book she wanted.

In the beginning, Julia Gillian had loved the green book. There was a boy in it and his old dog and the boy's grandfather. The grandfather and the boy built a tree house, and they made a pulley system with a large basket so that the boy could haul the dog up and down at will. Julia Gillian was taken with that phrase: "At will."

It had seemed that, finally, she had found a book she could love.

But then, thirty-six pages in, a feeling had come over her: *This book is not going to turn out well.* Given her powers of knowing, Julia Gillian had not even tried to talk herself out of this feeling. Since she had no wish to read a book with an unhappy ending, she had immediately closed the green book and decided never to open it again.

That had not been enough, however. When Julia Gillian looked at the green book, which stood on a shelf beside her bed, she felt frightened. The words were still in there. They could be read at any time. There was no guarantee that, at some point, she might not find herself opening the book and reading on, on to the ending that she strongly suspected would not be happy.

Julia Gillian had even removed the ponytail holders from her hair, both the blue one and the yellow one, and strung them around the book.

"There," she had said to Bigfoot. "That should do the trick."

But the ponytail holders had not done the trick. The green book was still there, still sitting on the bookshelf beside her bed. Now she felt caught between her parents and their unhappy newspaper in the kitchen, and the green book with its potentially unhappy ending in her room. What should she do?

She decided to put on a mask of her own creation. She was highly skilled at the art of balloon + papier-mâché masks. Over time, Julia Gillian had developed her own special recipe for flour and water paste. She had then memorized it, so that whenever the urge struck she could whip up a papier-mâché mask.

Julia Gillian kept her masks in a large cardboard

box with a lid. Now she lifted the lid and surveyed the contents. So many masks to choose from. Which one should she wear today? Perhaps the raccoon mask. She was especially fond of the raccoon mask, with the black and brown stripes she had painted on with her watercolors. The big, bold stripes, in combination with

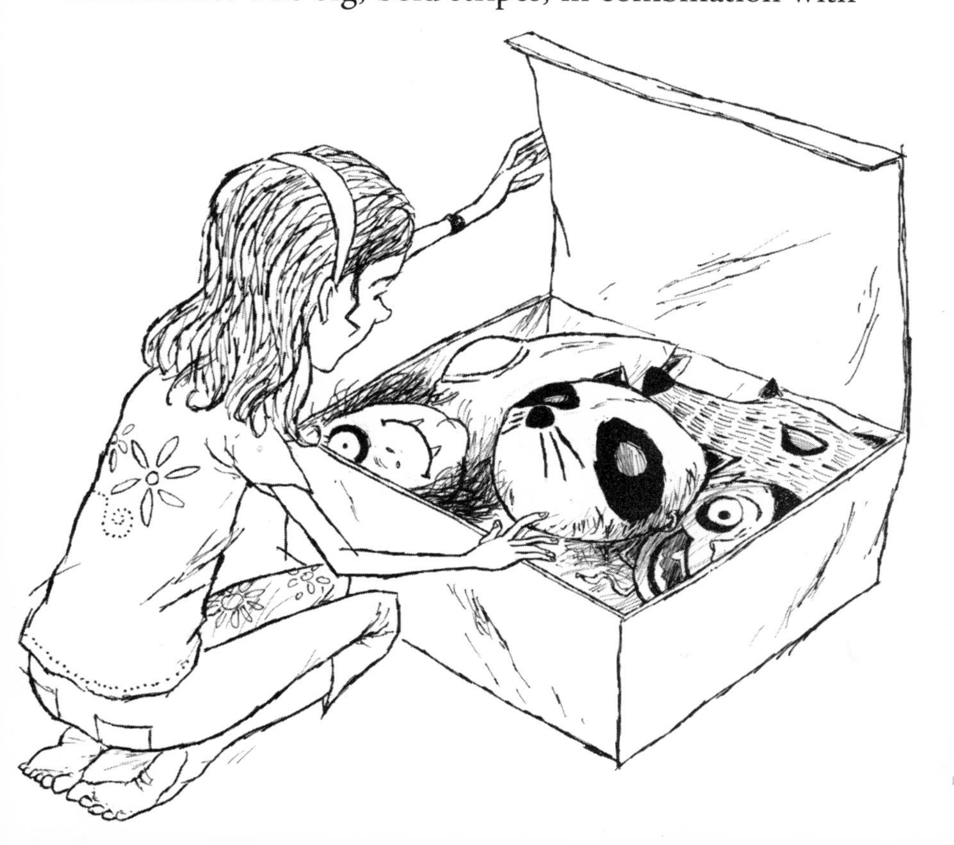

the serious black nose, made this raccoon an animal to reckon with. With the fierce raccoon mask tied on securely, Julia Gillian felt much safer. Indeed, she felt ready to conquer the wider world.

"Take that, budget cuts," said Julia Gillian. "Take that, global warming."

She double-knotted the shoelace strings of the mask for extra security. She preferred to use shoelaces on her masks, rather than rubber bands, because she had found that shoelaces were effective and readily available.

If she found herself in need of a shoelace, she could always borrow one from one of her shoes. Or, in a pinch, from one of her parents' shoes.

"What do you think, Bigfoot?"

Julia Gillian gazed down through the raccoon eyeholes so that Bigfoot could get the full effect of her fierceness. Bigfoot looked up and thumped his tail on the floor approvingly.

"Thanks. Let's go see Percy."

At the mention of Percy, Bigfoot's eyes widened and his tongue hung out. As far as Bigfoot was concerned, Percy, a smallish black dog who lived in a mustard-colored house with a white picket fence down the block, could do no wrong. This made Julia Gillian sad, because it was obvious that Percy did not feel the same way about Bigfoot. She had observed that Percy looked with disdain at Bigfoot, as if his cartoonishly large size somehow made him a lesser dog. Percy himself was devoted to an old, nasty tennis ball, which Julia Gillian privately thought made him a lesser dog himself. But the tennis ball, which was usually clenched between Percy's jaws, did prevent him from barking, and that was just as well.

"Percy," Julia Gillian encouraged Bigfoot. "Yes, let's go see Percy!"

Although Percy had lived down the block from the Gillians for a year now and had never shown the slightest inclination to befriend Bigfoot, she still held out hope that someday, when she least expected it, the situation might change. How happy that would make Bigfoot. And anything that would make Bigfoot happy, Julia Gillian wanted.

Bigfoot hauled himself up from his long magenta pillow and she clipped the leash to his collar. There was no need of a leash with Bigfoot, as he would never think of straying from her side, but Minneapolis had strict leash laws and Julia Gillian was a law-abiding citizen. She tied a couple of plastic bags to the leash, just in case (Minneapolis also had strict dog-poop laws), and she and Bigfoot headed to the front door.

"Bye, sweetie," said her mother.

"Bye, honey," said her father. "We're taking a break from the books to go get some groceries. I'm not sure we'll be back in an hour, so check in with Enzo on your way out and again when you come home."

"Will do," said Julia Gillian.

"Will do" was a phrase that Julia Gillian had heard on the radio, and she was trying it on for size. Her parents raised their eyebrows at the sound of the new phrase, but they were used to their daughter trying out new phrases, and they made no comment.

This summer, Julia Gillian's parents were in summer school, but they were not teaching summer school. No, her parents were taking classes themselves. They were taking a double load of classes so that they could finish their graduate degrees sooner rather than later. Julia Gillian was not exactly sure what a graduate degree was, but she did know that the dining room table was covered with heavy books.

Given the summer heat, the overhead fan was usually on, which meant that the pages of those heavy books constantly flipped back and forth. Over the summer, Julia Gillian had become used to the *flip flip flip* sound of her parents' books. Occasionally this sound grated on her, and she weighted the pages down with the salt

and pepper shakers and fruit bowl, but her parents always forgot to re-weight the pages, and the *flip flip flip* began anew.

Now that she was nine, Julia Gillian was allowed to walk a nine-square-block area of the city streets for an entire hour without her parents, as long as Bigfoot was with her. She and Bigfoot closed the door behind them and walked down the long hallway and then down the stairs to the floor where Enzo lived. Enzo was eighteen years old, and she lived with her older brother, Zap, who was in his twenties and studying to be a chef at Dunwoody Culinary Institute. Sometimes Enzo babysat for Julia Gillian, but more often she acted as a backup for Julia Gillian's parents.

Secretly Julia Gillian was a bit jealous of Enzo and Zap because of their names. Though she loved her own name, in moments of great honesty she admitted to herself that she loved Enzo's and Zap's names more. Enzo had been named after her father, and Zap was called Zap because he loved superheroes.

"Don't you think that Zap and Enzo have perfect names?" Julia Gillian had once asked her parents, and her parents had agreed that Zap and Enzo were certainly not run-of-the-mill names, and that they were indeed perfect in their own unique way.

2A

CHAPTER THREE

Enzo

At Enzo's front door, Julia Gillian knocked her secret Enzo knock: three slow and loud with her left fist, three fast and light with her right fist, three medium with both fists, like this:

KNOCK. KNOCK. KNOCK.

KnockKnockKnock.

Knock. Knock. Knock.

"Come on in, Noodlie!" called Enzo from within.

Enzo had several nicknames for Julia Gillian. All of her nicknames sort of rhymed with "Julia," but only in a far-fetched sort of way. Noodlie was one of Julia Gillian's favorites, because Enzo used it when she felt especially filled with affection for her. Usually Julia Gillian would feel a rush of happiness at the sound of Enzo calling her Noodlie, but today that did not happen.

"Noodlie, oh, Noodlie," Enzo yodeled from within. "Where's my Noooooodlie?"

This yodel was the signal that Julia Gillian should open the door herself, because Enzo was feeling too lazy to get up and open the door. Julia Gillian fished out the key to Enzo's apartment, which she kept on a string around her neck along with the key to her own apartment, and opened the door. Enzo was lying in her indoor reading hammock. She had set herself the summer task of reading *The Collected Plays of William Shakespeare*, and consequently she was spending much of the summer lying in her indoor reading hammock, reading.

Enzo saw no reason why hammocks should be used only outside, and Julia Gillian agreed. She wished that she herself had a hammock in the living room instead of a couch, but her parents did not share her opinion.

An indoor reading hammock was the sort of thing you could have when you lived with your older brother and not your parents. Enzo was eighteen, which meant that she was legally an adult and she could choose where she wanted to live. Her parents worked the night shift, and Enzo liked company, so she chose to live with her brother. This situation had struck Julia Gillian as sad when she first heard about it. She herself would much prefer living with her parents. Then again, she did not have an older brother, especially

SHAKESPEARE
COMPLETE WORKS

one like Zap, and Enzo had assured her that she loved living with Zap. And Zap and Enzo always did seem happy in their apartment, which was filled with light and music and the indoor reading hammock and interesting baked goods of Zap's own creation.

Julia Gillian pushed her raccoon mask on top of her head. It was too hot to keep wearing it over her face, but as long as the fierce mask was attached to her head, she felt secure and able to conquer the wider world.

"Hey there, Noodlie," said Enzo. "Want to try a Zap creation of the day?"

She pointed at a dish of brownish squares on the dining room table. Zap frequently experimented with recipes of his own creation. Some of his recipes were tasty, and some were not. The tastiest ones ended up in the display case of the bakery on Hennepin Avenue, where he worked. Julia Gillian surveyed the brownish squares. They did not look appealing. No thank you to the Zap creation of the day.

"How's the Shakespeare going?" said Julia Gillian.

The enormous book lay facedown on Enzo's stomach.

"It's going."

"Enzo, do you ever read the newspaper?"

Julia Gillian had not expected that she would ask Enzo that question, but there it was.

"I read the comics sometimes," said Enzo. "Does that count?"

Julia Gillian thought about it. Did the comics count? She was not sure.

"Where are you headed?" said Enzo.

"For our walk. Mom and Dad said I should tell you I was leaving."

Suddenly Enzo was all business. She sat straight up, or as straight up as one could sit in a hammock.

"Remember your parameters," she said.

Enzo felt that she was not doing her babysitter duty unless she recited the rules every time Julia Gillian headed out with Bigfoot.

"Look both ways," said Enzo. "Don't talk to strangers, be back in no more than one hour, go no farther than nine square blocks, make sure Bigfoot gets some water because it's hot hot hot, and good luck with the claw machine."

"Got it," said Julia Gillian.

Enzo nodded once, a brisk we're-done-with-business nod. Enzo believed that young children in general were

SHAKESPEARE

capable of a great deal more than most adults gave them credit for. She believed in freedom and independence within bounds. Now she tapped the big man's watch that was always strapped to her wrist.

"You've got an hour," she said again. "Be back by nine forty-seven sharp. One minute past, and I call the police."

Julia Gillian nodded and pulled her raccoon mask back down over her face. Bigfoot strained at the leash.

"Hey, Noodlie," said Enzo. "Have you finished your green book?"

Julia Gillian shook her head. The raccoon mask scraped a little against the sides of her cheeks. She had not done a perfect job with the papier-mâché.

“That’s what I figured,” said Enzo. “The raccoon mask is your I-need-to-feel-brave mask, isn’t it?”

Julia Gillian nodded. Now the raccoon mask scraped against her forehead. Just a bit, but it was still annoying.

“Hang in there, Noodlie,” said Enzo. “Tell me what you’re going to remember for the next hour.”

“My parameters,” said Julia Gillian, and saluted.

“Good,” said Enzo. “Report back in fifty-nine minutes.”

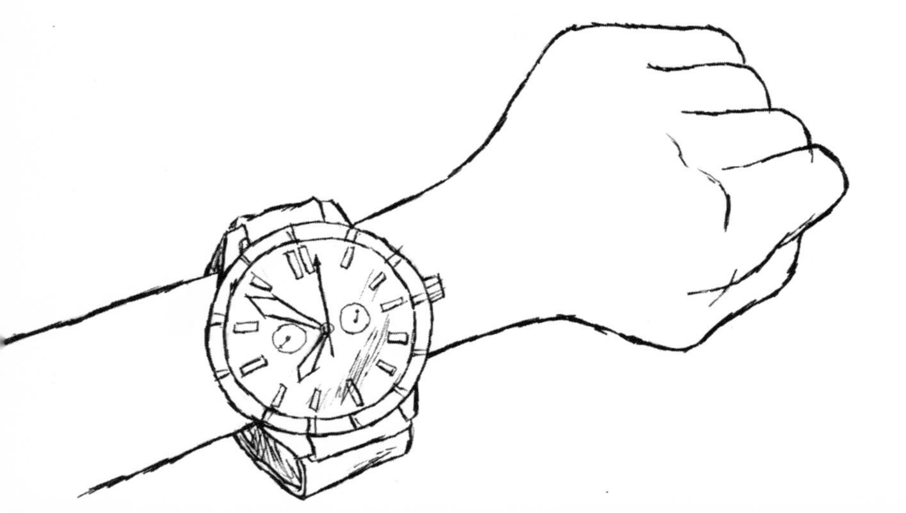

CHAPTER FOUR

Bryant Hardware

It was so hot outside that Julia Gillian wondered if an egg could actually be fried on the pavement. She had often heard this saying, and she decided that she would try it herself someday. Now she pushed her raccoon mask off her head so that it dangled down her back. She looked up to Enzo's window. Sure enough, Enzo was leaning out to make sure that Julia Gillian had made it safely to the sidewalk.

"Bye," called Julia Gillian.

Enzo gave her a salute of her own and disappeared into her apartment. Unlike Julia Gillian, Enzo was indeed a reader. Enzo was a reader who was not afraid

of books with unhappy endings. Julia Gillian knew this for a fact, because once, she had entered Enzo's apartment to find Enzo crying in her reading hammock. When Julia Gillian asked what was the matter, Enzo pointed to the book lying next to her, which she had just finished.

"It was such a good book," said Enzo.

"But you're crying."

"It had a sad ending."

"Sad endings are bad."

"Sad endings are neither bad nor good," said Enzo. "Sad endings just *are*."

Julia Gillian did not understand that at all, but she was nine and Enzo was eighteen, and maybe that made the difference. Was this what happened when you became a legal adult? Did books with sad endings become appealing?

Bigfoot tilted his head sideways and gave an experimental tug at the leash. He did not like it when Julia Gillian stood on the sidewalk, thinking. Now that he was outside, he wanted to get going.

"All right, Bigfoot," said Julia Gillian. "First we'll look for Percy, and then we'll pay a visit to the claw machine."

At the sound of his favorite dog's name, Bigfoot's ears pricked up and his tail began to wag. It was hard for Julia Gillian to witness Bigfoot's happiness, because she knew that Percy did not return Bigfoot's undying affection. Still, as she always reminded herself, things could change, and so she and Bigfoot started down the block in the direction of Percy's house. There he was, out in his minuscule front yard.

"Hello, Percy," said Julia Gillian.

Percy ignored her. How typical. He tossed his ratty tennis ball in the air and scrabbled around for it with his front paws. Bigfoot panted and whined. His tail thumped on the hot pavement, but Percy did not even glance in his direction.

Then Julia Gillian did something mean.

"Going to the dog park, Percy?" she said.

At this, Percy leaped up and ran over to the fence.

He jumped and wiggled, his brown eyes frantic with excitement. There was nothing that Percy loved more than the dog park, and Julia Gillian knew it. It was mean of her to say the words *dog park* to Percy, who was confined to his front yard. But she said it anyway, because she was tired of Percy ignoring her dog.

"No dog park for you today, Percy. That's what you get for not being nice to Bigfoot."

Bigfoot trotted obediently beside Julia Gillian, but she could tell that his heart was really back in Percy's front yard.

"Percy doesn't like you the way you like him," said Julia Gillian to Bigfoot. "I'm sorry, but it's true."

Bigfoot looked downcast. He didn't slow his pace, but dejection was on his face.

"That might change," Julia Gillian told him. "But in the meantime, you've got bigger fish to fry than that little snobby dog."

Bigfoot kept trotting. He was such a good dog, and it made Julia Gillian angry that Percy didn't love him the way he deserved to be loved. She decided to change the subject.

"I tell you what," said Julia Gillian to Bigfoot. "Let's go check out the claw machine."

Not many people in Minneapolis knew about the claw machine, which was hidden away in the back of Bryant Hardware on 36th Street. Julia Gillian had found it years ago on a day when her mother was occupied at the front of the store with paint swatches. Bryant Hardware was a small store across the street from Our Kitchen, where her father sometimes took her for pancakes. She liked to examine the front display window of Bryant Hardware whenever she passed by, because the display window, like Julia Gillian, was skilled in the art of knowing.

Toward the end of summer, the front window featured rakes and leaf bags, with large, colored construction-paper maple leaves taped up to the top part of the glass. Each year Julia Gillian wondered who cut out the paper maple leaves. Was it Mr. Bryant Senior himself? She herself was good at cutting out construction paper leaves. Construction paper flowers, too.

And a few weeks before Halloween, the window

was filled with rubber masks and a witch riding a broom. Over the years, the witch's warty nose had become battered. If Julia Gillian peered closely, she could see where the nose had been restuck to the witch's face with duct tape. The rubber masks in the window were not like the masks that she was good at making. These Bryant Hardware masks were extremely frightening. Julia Gillian had once witnessed identical twins, dressed in identical yellow outfits and riding in a double stroller, stare at the rubber Halloween masks and then burst into tears at exactly the same moment.

As she and Bigfoot neared the store, Julia Gillian decided to practice the art of knowing.

"It's summer, right?" she said to Bigfoot. "So the

window will probably be filled with swim toys and pails and shovels."

Bigfoot looked up and tilted his head, which was his way of saying that he agreed. Bigfoot was almost always agreeable. Once they were in front of Bryant Hardware, Julia Gillian saw that she was right again. There they were: swim toys, pails, and plastic shovels.

"We did it again," Julia Gillian said to Bigfoot.

Bigfoot wagged his tail happily.

"Maybe this is a good sign, Bigfoot. Maybe this means that today we'll win at the claw machine."

BRYANT
HARDWARE
OPEN

CHAPTER FIVE

Meerkat, Come to Me

The door to Bryant Hardware had swollen in the sticky summer heat, but Julia Gillian threw her weight behind it.

"Well, hello, Miss Gillian," said Mr. Bryant Senior. "How's my girl and her tiny dog this fine day?"

"Your girl and her tiny dog are good, thanks," said Julia Gillian.

She could hear her English teacher father in the back of her mind, telling her that she should say *fine* instead of *good*, but she ignored him. Mr. Bryant Senior and Julia Gillian had a long-running joke between themselves. Mr. Bryant Senior referred to Bigfoot as Julia Gillian's tiny dog, and so did Julia Gillian. Mr. Bryant Senior asked a question, and Julia Gillian parroted his question as her response. Bigfoot thumped his tail. Suddenly Julia Gillian wondered if Bigfoot had any idea how enormous he was. Did dogs have a sense of their own size? She had never considered this question before.

"Are you heading to the claw machine?" said Mr. Bryant Senior.

She nodded.

"Well, look what I just found. I believe these belong to you, Miss Gillian."

He handed her two quarters.

Mr. Bryant Senior and Julia Gillian had

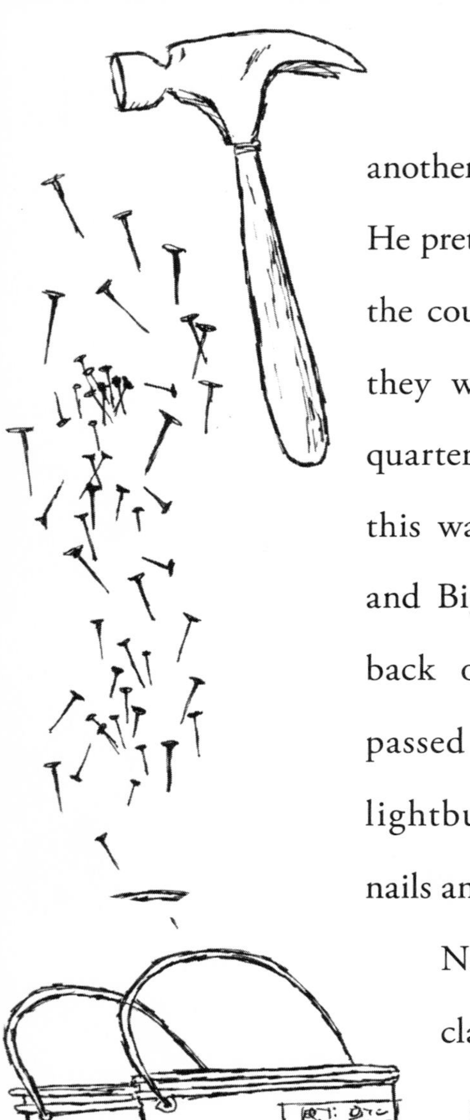

another long-running understanding. He pretended to find two quarters on the counter, and she pretended that they were hers. Since it cost two quarters to play the claw machine, this was a good deal. Julia Gillian and Bigfoot made their way to the back of Bryant Hardware. They passed the paint swatches, the lightbulbs, and the assorted nails and screws.

Now they stood before the claw machine, which was red and square and much taller than Julia Gillian. She placed her quarters into the quarter slots. She checked to see that the meerkat was still in the upper left-hand corner of the machine. Very few people knew of the claw machine's existence, and according to Mr. Bryant Senior, weeks went by without anyone but Julia Gillian using it, but still, she wanted to make sure that nothing had changed.

TOY
PARADE

"Today might be our day, Bigfoot," said Julia Gillian.

Bigfoot did not wag his tail or tilt his head. He was used to the claw machine routine, and he waited patiently for the routine to be over.

Julia Gillian closed her eyes and said her claw machine mantra three times:

Meerkat meerkat, come to me.

Meerkat meerkat, come to me.

Meerkat meerkat, come to me.

Then she pushed in the quarters and held her breath as the claw machine whirred to life. Bells clanged and lights flashed and the claw opened and closed three times. Julia Gillian maneuvered the levers until the claw was directly over the meerkat. Then she pressed the button. She watched as the claw descended in its jerky way, brushed the edge of the meerkat's ear, and closed on thin air.

Empty.

Julia Gillian sighed and pulled off her racoon mask. She wanted that meerkat more than anything. She had wanted that meerkat ever since the first day she had seen it, back when she was six years old, on the day her mother had been trying to choose paint colors. Ever since then, she had tried, on Sundays and Fridays, to win the meerkat. The meerkat would be the perfect companion to Julia Gillian's stuffed whistling marmot, which sat on her bed in a place of honor, and with which she slept

every night. Julia Gillian was convinced that with time and practice, she would master the art of the claw. After all, she was good at many things. But it had been three years now, and she was not yet a claw master.

"Someday we'll get the meerkat, Bigfoot," said Julia Gillian. "I promise."

Bigfoot thumped his tail hard. The familiar claw machine routine was over and he was anxious to get back on the road. They returned to the front of the store, where Mr. Bryant Senior had just finished ringing up a large order of paint trays, rollers, and three cans of "Rhubarb Tart" paint for a portly man wearing white overalls. On the newspaper rack next to the cash register were the headlines, some of which included the unhappy words: *global warming, budget cuts, war.*

Julia Gillian sighed again. Another Sunday claw

machine attempt had come and gone, and she was still meerkat-less. Suddenly she was not sure that she was, in fact, ready to take on the wider world. She pulled the raccoon mask down over her face again. The fierce stripes of the raccoon mask would give her strength.

"Harvey, this is Miss Gillian and her tiny dog," said Mr. Bryant Senior to the portly white-overall man.

Harvey stared at the masked Julia Gillian. Then he stared at the not-tiny Bigfoot. Harvey shook his head, picked up his bags, and left.

"Maybe Harvey doesn't like raccoons," said Mr. Bryant Senior.

Mr. Bryant Senior and Julia Gillian looked at each

other. Mr. Bryant Senior smiled and so did Julia Gillian, underneath her raccoon mask.

"Where are my girl and her tiny dog off to now, Miss Gillian?"

"Your girl and her tiny dog are going home now, Mr. Bryant Senior."

"We'll see you on Friday then, Miss Gillian."

"Indeed you will, Mr. Bryant Senior," said Julia Gillian.

CHAPTER SIX

Dogs! Please Help Yourselves!

It was important that Julia Gillian remember her parameters and be back by 9:47 a.m., not one minute later, or Enzo would call the police. Julia Gillian had never been late, so Enzo had never had reason to call the police, but Julia Gillian had no doubt that Enzo *would* call the police. That was the kind of person Enzo was. She was as quietly fierce in real life as Julia Gillian felt when she was wearing her raccoon mask. She pushed her mask back on her head and took a deep breath of non-mask air.

"Let's get a move on, Bigfoot. Or else Enzo might call the police."

Bigfoot let his tongue hang out. He was hot and tired, but still, he picked up the pace. He would do anything for Julia Gillian. She was his favorite person in all the world.

"Are you the dog of my dreams, Bigfoot?" said Julia Gillian. "Yes, you are."

Sometimes Julia Gillian talked to Bigfoot in a puppy voice, like just now, but only when no one else was around to hear. Now she tugged at Bigfoot's leash ever so slightly, just enough to let him know that they were going to turn left on 35th and Girard Avenue. This was a detour, but not much of one, and Julia Gillian felt confident that they would still make it home within their parameters. A kind person who lived halfway down the Girard Avenue block often left a bowl of water out on hot days. The kind Girard Avenue person, whom Julia Gillian had never met, kept the bowl filled with water and propped a little sign up next to it: DOGS! PLEASE HELP YOURSELVES!

The DOGS! PLEASE HELP YOURSELVES! sign had been laminated, so that it would last forever, through rain and mist and hail and snow. Julia Gillian loved lamination. Someday she hoped to master the art of lamination. She pictured all the things that she could then laminate if she wanted to: birthday cards, abstract portraits, excellent spelling quizzes, and all manner of signs. Lamination was a wonderful thing. Sometimes, when Julia Gillian's parents were sighing over their newspaper, she wanted to remind them that there were many good things in the world, such as lamination.

The DOGS! PLEASE HELP YOURSELVES! sign was propped against the base of the kind Girard Avenue person's birch tree. The bowl, which was blue with little black-enamel paw prints, was filled with water.

"Dog!" said Julia Gillian, in an exclamation-mark kind of voice. "Please help yourself!"

Bigfoot looked up at her with a slightly annoyed expression. He was used to Julia Gillian wearing masks of her own creation, but he did not like it when she used her exclamation-mark voice.

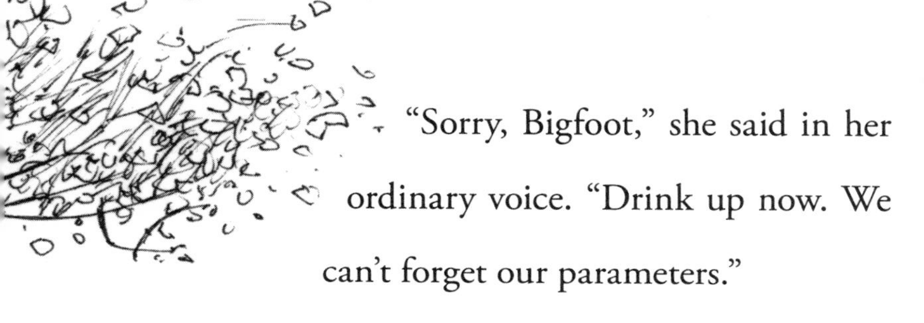

"Sorry, Bigfoot," she said in her ordinary voice. "Drink up now. We can't forget our parameters."

Bigfoot bent his head to the paw-print bowl and drank. When he was finished, the water was nearly gone. The kind Girard Avenue person who lived in the house behind the birch tree would have to refill it now, but that was all right. Bigfoot was not being greedy. Bigfoot was just being a dog, and the kind Girard Avenue person obviously loved dogs. Bigfoot lifted his dripping head and gave himself a small shake.

"Good boy, Bigfoot," said Julia Gillian.

They continued on their way, picking up the pace just a little so as to be sure to make it home with a few minutes to spare.

"Bigfoot, what do you think of my green book?" said Julia Gillian.

Sometimes she liked to ask her dog questions about troublesome matters. The green book, bound with ponytail holders and sitting on her bookshelf, qualified as a troublesome matter. In answer to her question, Bigfoot wagged his tail. That was his usual response, and Julia Gillian found it encouraging. She kept going.

"Because I'm worried that the ending will be unhappy. I'm worried about the dog."

Bigfoot stopped wagging his tail. Maybe he was too hot to wag, or maybe he too suspected that the ending was not a happy one. Julia Gillian considered whether or not she should reveal her deepest suspicion about the ending to Bigfoot. She was afraid even to think too much about the possibly sad ending of the green book, but the more she didn't think about it, the more she ended up thinking about it.

"What I'm really worried about," said Julia Gillian, "is that the dog might die."

There. She had said the words. Now they were out in the open, hanging in the air between her and her dog. Bigfoot gave one brisk wag of his tail and trotted steadily on. He did not seem upset at hearing Julia Gillian's prediction. Of course, he was a dog, and therefore did not know what the word *die* meant.

"Bigfoot?"

Bigfoot heard the question in her voice and turned his head up to her.

"I'm not just worried," said Julia Gillian. "I'm scared."

They had reached the front steps of their apartment building. Enzo was peering down from her window, tapping the heavy man's wristwatch on her arm and frowning.

"Only two minutes to spare, Poodle," came Enzo's voice from inside. "That's cutting it pretty close, you know."

Poodle was a nickname that Enzo reserved for times of tension. But two minutes to spare was still two minutes to spare. The day had not yet come to pass in which Julia Gillian was late coming home, and Enzo knew it, so there was really no reason to bring out the Poodle nickname. Julia Gillian stroked the fur directly behind Bigfoot's ear, where it was softest.

"I'm scared, Bigfoot," said Julia Gillian again.

She felt a small rush inside her, as if the air inside one of her papier-mâché balloon molds had been released. She had spoken the truth, and now Bigfoot knew her secret.

"Should we go in?"

Julia Gillian looked down at Bigfoot and tilted her head so that he would tilt his. This was one of the things she most loved about her dog: the way he mirrored her own movements.

CHAPTER SEVEN

The Bakery

It was Monday morning, and the unhappy newspaper had been read, the sighs had been sighed, the toast had been buttered and eaten, and Julia Gillian's parents were now sitting at the dining table. Piles of papers and piles of books surrounded them, and each was scribbling on yellow lined pads.

"Why are you taking summer school classes?" said Julia Gillian.

"Because we want to be great teachers," said her father.

"Yes," agreed her mother. "We want to be the best teachers in the history of the world."

They did not even look up from their piles of books, perhaps because Julia Gillian had asked this very question nearly every morning of the summer.

"But you're already great teachers," said Julia Gillian.

This much she knew from walking around south Minneapolis with them. Every few blocks, it seemed, another elementary schooler ran up to her mother and gave her a hug, or another high schooler sauntered up to her father and slapped his hand and said, "Yo, Gillian." Julia Gillian was not jealous of these other children, because she had her mother and father all to herself, and not just as teachers, but as parents.

"There's always room for improvement," said her father.

Julia Gillian supposed this must be true. Her father certainly said it often. But this summer was not the way most summers were for the Gillian family. There had been few trips to the water park this year, and none to the Oliver Kelley Living History Farm. What's more, Julia Gillian had not eaten a cucumber sandwich or seen the red-and-white-checked tablecloth since the last day of school, which was the last time she and her parents had taken a picnic to the Rose Garden. Her father had not knit a single fluffy multicolored scarf in preparation for Christmas gift giving, nor had her mother made a single birdhouse to give away to the residents of the Walker Senior Center.

Instead, each day Julia Gillian's parents bent over their books, taking breaks to quiz each other on teaching pedagogy. She had no idea what teaching pedagogy was, but her parents certainly worked hard at it.

No, this was not a typical summer. This was, instead, the summer of nine-square-block walks. It was the summer of Enzo reminding Julia Gillian to remember her parameters. It was the summer of frequent wearing of the raccoon papier-mâché mask. It was the summer of the green book, sitting silent and closed on her bookshelf. It was the summer when Julia Gillian admitted to her dog that she was scared. Was this what happened when you turned nine and began to grow up?

"Where are you and Bigfoot heading today, sweetie?" said her mother.

"Here and there."

"Here and there specifically where?"

Julia Gillian sighed.

"To the bakery."

"Be sure to check in with Enzo," said her father.

"Indeed I will," said Julia Gillian.

KNOCK. KNOCK. KNOCK.

KnockKnockKnock.

Knock. Knock. Knock.

Enzo was in her indoor reading hammock. Was it possible that Enzo had barely moved in the two days since Julia Gillian had last seen her? She had propped a fan up on the dining table so that it blew directly on her.

"Are you hungry, Noodlie?" said Enzo. "Because if you are, there's a Zap creation of the day on the table."

Julia Gillian was not hungry, but she inspected the Zap creation anyway. Zap's creations of the day were interesting to look at, even if she did not always want to try them. This particular creation of the day was purple, with a bit of green and gray.

"Well," said Julia Gillian. "I'm just checking in. Bigfoot and I should go now."

"What are you going to remember?"

"My parameters."

Enzo tapped her heavy watch. "Fifty-nine minutes from now. Go."

On the way out, Julia Gillian admired the neat row of shoes outside Enzo and Zap's door. Theirs was a shoe-free household. Enzo liked neatness, and she liked to line up her shoes and Zap's shoes precisely. Enzo's shoes were small and narrow, like Enzo herself, but Zap's shoes were like miniature boats. Although Zap was not enormous, his shoes were size 15. Julia Gillian liked to quiz herself, so she studied them: black high-tops, gray Velcro sandals, and brown lace-ups. Which shoes were missing?

Flip-flops. Yes, that must be what Zap was wearing today in the bakery. The largest flip-flops in the world, and bright red.

Julia Gillian looked again at Zap's brown lace-ups. They were such big shoes, and her own feet were so

small in comparison. Zap was tall and brave and always laughing. He struck Julia Gillian as fearless, and she had a sudden urge to step inside his shoes. Perhaps his bravery would rub off on her.

Bigfoot looked. He was a patient dog, but Julia Gillian could tell that he was also anxious to get going.

"Okay, Bigfoot," said Julia Gillian. "We'll go see Zap now."

She looked up and down the hallway and then carefully stepped into Zap's brown lace-ups. It was as she had predicted; her feet in their orange sandals fit

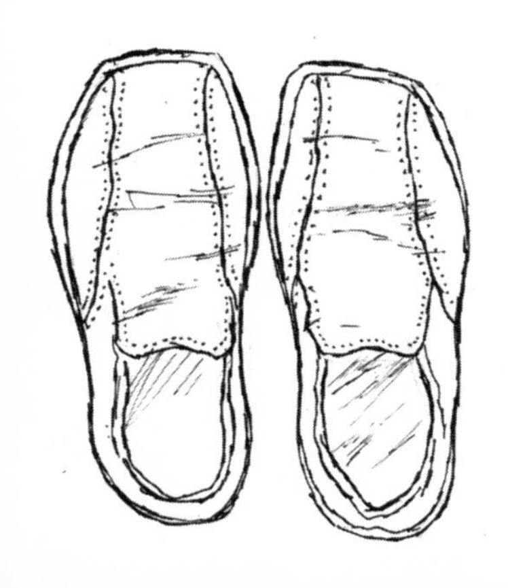

entirely inside. Julia Gillian slipped her feet out of the enormous shoes without disturbing them, there was that much room to spare. Did she feel braver now? She might. It was a little hard to tell.

She clipped the leash onto Bigfoot's collar, and off they went. Today was even hotter than yesterday. Her parents blamed global warming for the hot days, and said that the worst was yet to come. Julia Gillian looked around her, at her block of Emerson Avenue. The trees were deepest green now, at the height of summer, and the sky was a white-blue, and the puffy clouds drifting by were like the kind of clouds that she used to finger-paint in kindergarten. When the worst that was yet to come came, what would happen?

Julia Gillian wished she were at the Quang Vietnamese Restaurant, drinking a strawberry bubble tea. But she was not at the Quang. She was outside on the hot pavement.

"I'm sorry, Bigfoot," she said. "But we need to go back upstairs and get something."

Bigfoot's head drooped a bit, but since he was a patient dog who trusted her completely, he let her lead him back up to the apartment. Julia Gillian retrieved her fierce raccoon mask from her bedpost, where it had been watching over her all day and all night. She slipped the mask over her head and let it dangle about her neck.

"*Now* we can go," said Julia Gillian, and Bigfoot's tail wagged briskly.

The snobby little Percy was nowhere to be seen today. Julia Gillian did not even glance at his mustard-colored house as they rounded the corner of the block, and surprisingly, neither did Bigfoot. Perhaps Percy was at the dog park, growling at any dog that came close to him and his ratty old tennis ball. The dog park was ten blocks outside Julia Gillian's allotted nine-square-block walk, so Bigfoot and Julia Gillian only went to the dog park when her parents were able to go with them. She realized that this was another thing that had changed this summer. There had been many fewer trips to the dog park.

The bakery was one open room on Hennepin Avenue, with ceiling fans and a black-and-white-tiled floor and big screened windows that opened onto the sidewalk. Bigfoot headed straight to the counter, where Zap was

juggling caramels. Zap was an excellent juggler. He had promised that whenever Julia Gillian wanted to learn how to juggle, he would teach her the art. She longed to learn the art of juggling, but she felt that she needed to master the claw machine first. That day had not yet come, and now Julia Gillian watched and admired the caramels flying through the air.

"Great mask, JG," said Zap. He was the only person in the world who called Julia Gillian "JG." "Cool stripes. Did you make it yourself?"

"Indeed I did."

"Good job. And hello, there's my Bigfoot. How are you today, my canine friend?"

Bigfoot's whole body trembled with his love for Zap, who always called him "my Bigfoot." Julia Gillian was not jealous of this, because she knew that Zap was just trying to make Bigfoot feel good. Julia Gillian could tell that Bigfoot wanted to heave himself up and place his paws on the counter, but Bigfoot was a well-trained dog and he resisted. Zap leaned over the counter so that he was closer to Bigfoot. Zap always spoke to Bigfoot in a normal human voice. He never used the high-pitched puppy voice that many people, sometimes even Julia Gillian herself, tended to use around dogs.

"Are you hungry, my Bigfoot? Would you like a treat?"

Bigfoot wagged his tail. Whatever Zap gave him, he would willingly eat.

"Here you go, then," said Zap.

Zap slid a bowl of brownish wafers across the counter to Julia Gillian, who took it and placed it on the floor in front of the display case. Bigfoot bent his head to the bowl.

Sniff. Gulp. Gulp.

The brownish wafers were gone.

"That's a recipe of my own creation," said Zap.

"Peanut butter, oatmeal, dried carrots, and just a tinch of cornmeal. I call them 'Bigfoot Wows.'"

At the sound of his name, Bigfoot looked up hopefully.

"He likes them," said Julia Gillian.

Translating Bigfoot language into human language was one of Julia Gillian's many talents. At the sound of her voice, Bigfoot wagged his tail.

"He *really* likes them," added Julia Gillian.

"Then he shall have more of them," said Zap. "That is my decree."

Zap was in charge of the food at the bakery, and if Zap decreed that Bigfoot Wows would be on the menu, then Bigfoot Wows would be on the menu.

"So, JG," said Zap. "Ready to learn how to juggle yet?"

"Not yet."

"Sunday was not a meerkat day for you?"

Julia Gillian shook her head. Zap knew that she was determined to master the art of the claw before she moved on to juggling. But Sunday had not been a meerkat day, and today was a global warming day, and at home, the ponytail holder–bound green book sat on her bookshelf. Julia Gillian felt a wave of tiredness. She pulled her raccoon mask down over her face and peered through the fierce eyeholes at Zap. Maybe if she had feet as big as Zap's, she would not be afraid.

"Friday is your next claw machine day, isn't it, JG?" said Zap. "Perhaps, this very Friday, the meerkat will finally be yours."

Julia Gillian nodded behind her mask. Then she tugged at Bigfoot's leash, and they headed home.

CHAPTER EIGHT
Shoelaces

On the way home from the bakery, Julia Gillian and Bigfoot passed by a redbrick house on Fremont Avenue. Julia Gillian admired redbrick houses, this one especially, because the family who lived there had installed a tetherball, and she loved that game. A small girl, perhaps five years old, with dark hair and big eyes, was often in the front yard playing tetherball, which was a game you could play with someone or by yourself.

Today, the little girl was not playing tetherball. She was sitting on the steps leading from the lawn to the sidewalk, and she looked worried. Her sneakers lay on the step beside her and she was staring down at her feet and wiggling her toes.

"Hello," said Julia Gillian.

"Hi."

"How are you today?"

"Okay."

"Just okay?"

Julia Gillian heard herself talking to the worried little girl in the same way a grownup would talk to a child. It was fun to talk like a grownup. She decided to keep it up.

"Is there a problem of some kind?"

"No."

"Are you sure?"

Julia Gillian crouched beside the little girl. Bigfoot took the opportunity to sit. He bent his head and rubbed his cheek on his leash, which was something he occasionally liked to do.

"Yes."

This little girl was certainly not very talkative. Now she reached down to her sneakers and plucked at the laces.

"Are you going to put your sneakers on?" said Julia Gillian.

"No."

Goodness. Did this little girl ever say anything besides hi, okay, yes, and no? Maybe she had been taught that she should never speak to anyone she didn't know well, even friendly older children out walking their friendly large dogs. Julia Gillian decided to keep trying anyway.

"Are you going to be going to school soon?"

"Yes."

"What grade are you going to be in?"

"Kindergarten."

The little girl did not look up at Julia Gillian. She kept plucking at the laces of her sneakers. Bigfoot lay down on the pavement and yawned.

"Are you looking forward to kindergarten?"

"No."

Was this what being a grownup was like? If so, it was not as much fun as Julia Gillian had thought it would be.

"Why not?"

"Because."

The little girl plucked at her laces again.

"Both the kindergarten teachers at Lake Harriet Elementary are really nice," said Julia Gillian. "There's no need to worry."

No answer. Pluck.

"I was afraid to go to kindergarten," said Julia Gillian.

Julia Gillian wasn't sure why she had just told the little girl she had been afraid to go to kindergarten. Still, she had said the words, and the little girl was looking up at her.

"Why?"

"Because."

"Because why?"

Julia Gillian did not really want to tell this little girl why she had been scared to go to kindergarten. In fact, she was a little embarrassed to remember how afraid she had been. But the little girl was looking up at her with those big dark eyes, and it did not seem fair to leave her without an answer.

"Well," said Julia Gillian, "if you really want to know, I was scared to go without my dog."

The little girl looked at Bigfoot, who had closed one eye.

"He's big," she said.

"Indeed he is."

"They don't allow dogs in kindergarten."

"Indeed they don't."

"They don't allow stuffed animals either."

This did not seem right to Julia Gillian. She distinctly remembered bringing in her stuffed whistling marmot for kindergarten show-and-tell. But Julia Gillian had been a kindergartner four long years ago, and things changed, didn't they? Nothing stayed the same. The little girl plucked at her shoelaces again. They were red, and they straggled over the sidewalk.

"And guess what else?" said the little girl. "You have to know how to tie your shoes when you go to kindergarten."

"You do?"

Again Julia Gillian was confused. Had she herself known how to tie her shoes when she went to kindergarten? Truly she could not remember for sure.

"Yes, you do," said the little girl. "And you can't ask for help. Ever. Never."

Now the little girl pushed at her sneakers with her bare feet. She pushed them so hard that the sneakers actually tumbled down the step and onto the sidewalk next to Bigfoot, who opened his one closed eye and glanced at them.

"Well, that doesn't sound right to me," said Julia Gillian in her grownup voice. "I'm sure you can ask the teacher for help."

The little girl shook her head.

"No, you can't. And if you can't tie your shoes yourself, you have to go to the sub-basement and miss your snack and miss playground time. And you might get locked in school all night long."

This was definitely wrong. Julia Gillian wanted to laugh at how wrong all this information was, but the look on the little girl's face was too worried.

"No, no, no," said Julia Gillian in a soothing pretend-grownup voice. "None of that will happen. You'll see. The kindergarten teachers are nice. And guess what?

I didn't know how to tie my shoes when I went to kindergarten!"

The little girl looked up at Julia Gillian. She gave her a long look, up and down. Then she narrowed her eyes.

"You're lying," she said.

Was Julia Gillian lying? She honestly did not know, but it was possible. She decided to sidestep the issue. Grownups often did that, and she was pretending to be a grownup. Privately Julia Gillian believed that sidestepping an issue could be viewed as lying, but there was no sense telling that to the little girl.

"Do you know how to tie your shoes?" she said to the little girl.

The little girl buried her head in her hands and

shook it back and forth. Oh dear. Here was the real problem.

"Don't worry for a minute," she said to the little girl. "I'll teach you."

But the little girl just shook her head back and forth. Julia Gillian suspected that she had given up.

"It's not that hard to learn," said Julia Gillian. "Honestly."

Shake. Bigfoot raised his head and looked at the little girl, curled up around her knees, shaking her head. Then he looked at Julia Gillian, who did not know what to do. Where were this little girl's parents? Why were they not teaching her how to tie her shoes? Suddenly Julia Gillian did not want to be a grownup, even a pretend grownup, anymore.

"Everything will be all right," said Julia Gillian. "I promise."

In fact, Julia Gillian did not know if everything would be all right, but she wanted to help the little girl feel better. Just then, the little girl's father came out of their house and down to where his daughter was sitting sadly on the front steps.

Thank goodness. A real grownup had arrived.

"Hello there," he said to Julia Gillian.

He looked at her above his daughter's head and mouthed the words, *Scared to go to kindergarten.* Then he gave Julia Gillian the kind of look that grownups usually gave each other, a you-know-what-I-mean kind of look. *Thank you,* he mouthed. Julia Gillian nodded as if she were a grownup, too, even though she secretly was relieved to be done with pretending to be a grownup. It had not been the pleasant experience she had imagined.

CHAPTER NINE

Bigfoot the Babysitter

Back at home, Julia Gillian got out her box of papier-mâché masks and examined them: the King Tut mask, the praying mantis mask, the friendly-happy-child-ghost mask, the friendly-happy-child-vampire mask. Julia Gillian had originally intended to make her ghost and vampire masks terrifying, but after witnessing the fear of the twins outside Bryant Hardware, she had changed her mind.

Julia Gillian had nine masks in her collection, although they were not all the same

level of quality. When she first began making masks, she had not been skilled. In her collection was a blue mask, a yellow mask, and a red mask, all of which Julia Gillian thought of as her training masks. These training masks were almost flat, with small lumpy noses and eye slits that were not evenly spaced. It had been nearly impossible to see out of those first masks, not to mention how heavy they were.

Julia Gillian's mask-making ability had changed once she had the idea of draping her papier-mâché strips over blown-up balloons. Her first balloon papier-mâché mask had been extremely poofy, so much so that when she put it on and looked sideways in the mirror, her head appeared to be the size and shape of a basketball. Interesting, but not practical. Julia Gillian still kept this mask, as a reminder of how far she had come.

"I mastered the art of the basic mask long ago," said Julia Gillian to Bigfoot.

Bigfoot had followed her into her room and was turning around three times on his long magenta pillow. This was his pre-lying down ritual.

"But it'll be a long time before I am a true mask artist," said Julia Gillian. "That's because I have high standards."

Bigfoot wagged his tail. It was true that Julia Gillian's standards were high, and she saw no reason to lower them. In this way she was like Zap, who wanted to be the best chef in the state, the country, and the universe. And she was also like her parents, who wanted to be the best teachers in the history of the entire world. And she was like the Quang Vietnamese Restaurant, which made the best egg rolls in all of Minneapolis. They were tasty, crisp, and fresh, and Julia Gillian looked forward to them all week long.

Her high standards did not stop Julia Gillian from giving credit where credit was due. That was why she had added the Art of Papier-Mâché to her list of accomplishments. The day had come when she surveyed her array of basic masks and nodded in satisfaction.

"Time to add to the list," she had said to Bigfoot.

He had watched as Julia Gillian shoved up on the corner of her mattress and extracted her notebook. Back then, her list of accomplishments had covered only half of one side of a single sheet. What a long way she had come since then. And yet she was still waiting for the day when she could call herself a true mask artist.

Enzo, too, had high standards. Take her summer reading, for example. Enzo was not a good student in general, but she knew and loved her books. Julia Gillian, on the other hand, did not. This was an ongoing concern to her parents, both of whom believed there was no finer sight than a child with her legs draped over an easy chair, reading a good book.

"You just haven't found the right book yet," Enzo used to tell Julia Gillian.

Then came the green book. At first, Julia Gillian had thought that her reading curse had finally been broken. The boy, the dog, the pulley basket, and the tree house: Julia Gillian had been enchanted. But then she kept reading, and realized that the dog in the green book was old and lame. He was losing his hearing and perhaps even a bit of his sight. By page thirty-seven, it had become hard for him to climb into the pulley basket. That was when Julia Gillian had stopped reading. The dog in the green book was only one year older than

Bigfoot. If the green-book dog was old and lame and deaf, what did that mean for Bigfoot? Julia Gillian did not want to consider the possibilities.

Bigfoot had been born a few months before Julia Gillian. Her parents liked to tell the story of how, when they brought Julia Gillian home from the hospital as a newborn, Bigfoot had stood directly over her, all four paws planted firmly on the ground, and not allowed anyone but her parents to come near her.

"Bigfoot was your guardian angel," said her mother.

"He wasn't going to let anything harm you," said her father. "We used to leave you alone with Bigfoot and go out dancing until the wee hours, and we knew you would be perfectly fine."

"In no time at all that dog had learned how to give you a bottle and change your diapers."

"He even knew how to burp you. And that's a good thing, because you were a real burper."

Julia Gillian's parents liked to tell her stories of the many nights when Bigfoot had been her babysitter. How loyal and devoted he was, especially during the three days' blizzard when the power went out and Julia Gillian's parents had been stranded in Chicago.

A thought now occurred to Julia Gillian. She looked at Bigfoot, sleeping on his long magenta pillow. Although she had never questioned her parents' Bigfoot babysitting stories, she was suddenly suspicious. Was it truly possible that her parents had left her, a newborn, home alone with a Saint Bernard puppy?

Julia Gillian marched into the kitchen, where her parents were sitting at the table surrounded with their books and the papers. Summer school, summer school, summer school. Was that all they ever thought about?

"Mom," said Julia Gillian. "Dad. I have a question for you."

"Have you been lying to me all this time about Bigfoot being my babysitter?"

Her parents looked surprised. Neither said anything for a minute. They looked at each other, then they looked back at Julia Gillian. Then they both spoke at once.

"Honey —" said her father.

"Sweetie —" said her mother.

The answer was on their faces, and it was in the tentative sound of their voices.

"We thought you knew we were just joking," said her father.

"Well," said Julia Gillian. "I didn't."

Back in her bedroom, Julia Gillian sat down next to Bigfoot. This was the problem with getting older.

You realized that some things you had always taken for granted were not, in fact, the way you thought they were. Grownups did not always tell the truth. They might think they were just joking, but children took them seriously.

Maybe Julia Gillian should have known that her parents were lying to her. After all, they had lied to her once before, when she was five years old and informed them that she would not be going to kindergarten.

"But honey, why not?" her mother had said. "Kindergarten is fun!"

Julia Gillian's mother was a first-grade teacher at Kenwood Elementary. But first grade was not kindergarten, was it? And Kenwood Elementary was not Lake Harriet Elementary, was it? This meant that her mother could not know for sure that kindergarten, at Lake Harriet, for Julia Gillian, was going to be any fun at all.

"Nothing is more fun than kindergarten," her father had said.

Julia Gillian had ignored her father. He was a high school teacher. What could he know about kindergarten? The summer had marched on, with Julia Gillian steadfastly refusing to go to kindergarten and her parents gradually growing a bit panicky in their attempts to convince her how fun it would be.

"Honey, does your not wanting to go to kindergarten have to do with the fact that dogs can't go to kindergarten?" her mother had finally said.

And she had been right. Julia Gillian, at five years old, could not imagine going anywhere without her dog. Even when she and her parents went to the Quang Vietnamese Restaurant, they brought Bigfoot. They tied his leash to the tree outside the patio, and he waited patiently for them to finish, occasionally lapping up some of the water from the bowl that the kind Quang owners brought out to him.

"Yes," said Julia Gillian.

Her mother looked at her. Julia Gillian looked right back. She was not going to kindergarten without Bigfoot, and that was that.

"Well," said her mother slowly. "You might not know this, but you can bring Bigfoot to kindergarten."

What?

"That's right, honey," said her father. "You can bring Bigfoot to kindergarten."

Julia Gillian could still hear her parents' voices saying those words. They were the words that had gotten her to kindergarten, her new blue backpack strapped over her shoulders, Bigfoot walking ahead of her on his leash. But when they arrived at the school, and she had met her teacher and been shown her cubby, her mother and father had taken Bigfoot back home.

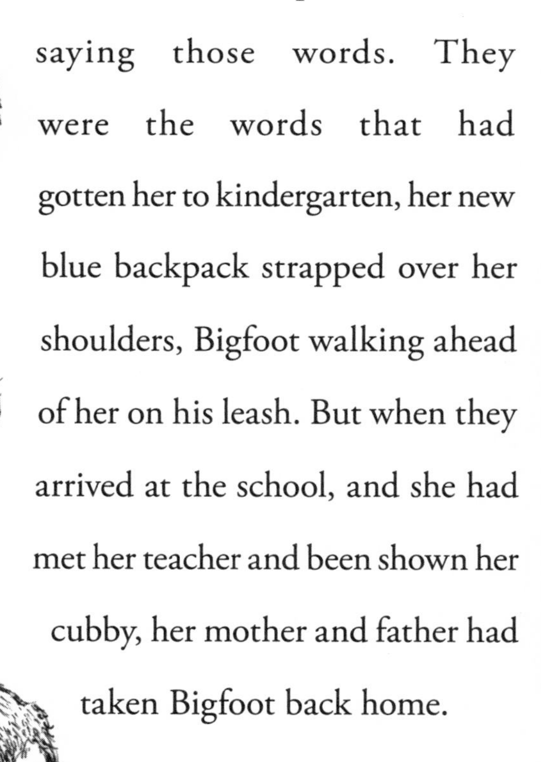

That night, Julia Gillian had cried to her parents.

"But honey, I didn't lie," said her mother. "Not really."

"That's right," said her father. "You did bring Bigfoot to kindergarten. He just couldn't stay, that's all."

That was what grownups called sidestepping the issue. But how was it different from a lie? Now that she was nine, Julia Gillian understood that her parents had been a little desperate to get her to kindergarten. While she didn't really blame them for what they had done, and even though her parents had not been lying about kindergarten itself — it was indeed fun, with

the pet guinea pig and the maple-leaf name tags and the cinnamon graham crackers at snack time — it was nevertheless a fact that Julia Gillian did not have good memories of her first, Bigfoot-less, day of kindergarten.

Julia Gillian sat on her bed thinking about sidestepping, lying, and girls who were afraid to be without their dogs. Down on his long magenta pillow, Bigfoot opened one eye and gazed up at her. He knew that something was wrong.

"Never mind, Bigfoot," Julia Gillian said. "You *could* have been my babysitter."

CHAPTER TEN

Pretending to Be Asleep

When Julia Gillian woke up early Tuesday morning, Bigfoot was already up and wagging his tail next to her. He wanted to go outside. It was Julia Gillian's job to take him out every morning to pee, but sometimes she was not in the mood. Sometimes, she just wanted to stay in bed. Today was one of those days.

"Soon, Bigfoot," she whispered to her dog.

Julia Gillian decided to practice her hearing for just a minute before she got out of bed. While she had excellent hearing, she did not want to take any chances. Practice made perfect, after all, and extra-sharp hearing was a good thing. She closed her eyes and focused.

She could hear her mother in the kitchen, slicing bread. It was almost impossible to hear someone slicing bread in the kitchen, and she was pleased at her ability to detect such a subtle sound.

Now for her father. Julia Gillian listened until she heard him leave the bathroom and start back down the hall. Now he was nearing her bedroom. She tried to smooth out her face so that she would look like an innocent child who badly needed to sleep instead of take her dog out to pee.

Her father's footsteps came down the hall. Now he paused outside her door. Now he looked in. Julia Gillian used her skills in the art of knowing to predict what would happen next.

Dad will see me sleeping and not want to wake me up.

Julia Gillian breathed slowly and softly, as if she were indeed asleep.

Dad will decide that just this once, he'll let me sleep, and he'll take Bigfoot out himself.

Julia Gillian kept her eyes shut, but not squinched. Squinched eyes were a dead giveaway in someone pretending to be asleep.

Dad will crook his finger at Bigfoot but not make a sound because he doesn't want to wake me up.

Julia Gillian shifted her head ever so slightly and sighed softly, the way people do when they are dreaming a pleasant dream from which they should not be waked.

Bigfoot will get up and follow Dad into the hallway.

Aha! Julia Gillian heard the *click click* of Bigfoot's toenails on the wooden floor of her bedroom.

Snick. Click.

Using her excellent hearing, Julia Gillian deduced that the two locks of the front door were unlocked.

Clink.

Now the leash was off the hook. The front door creaked open. And shut.

Julia Gillian popped open her eyes. She had made it! Oddly, now that she did not have to get up, she wanted to get up. She turned over and flung off the quilt. Then she stretched both arms way up over her head and closed her eyes and, just for the fun of it, yawned a huge pretend yawn. When she opened her eyes, her mother was standing in the doorway.

"Oh," said Julia Gillian. "Hi, Mom. I just woke up."

Her mother smiled. There was something about the smile that made Julia Gillian slightly nervous.

"Where's Bigfoot?" she said.

"I think you know where Bigfoot is, Julia."

Oh dear. Her mother had called her "Julia" instead of "Julia Gillian." This was not a good sign. Julia Gillian tried to furrow her brow, as if she was confused, but her face would not cooperate. She felt a grin coming on. She tried to cover it with another pretend yawn, but that did not work either.

Her mother started to laugh.

"You are an incorrigible child, Julia Gillian," said her mother. "And you shirk your early morning duties with that dog far too often. But, given that you are in most other ways a marvel of a girl, I shall just this once forgive you."

Julia Gillian did not know what *incorrigible* or *shirk* meant, but her mother was smiling, which meant that she was not really angry. That was all that mattered.

CHAPTER ELEVEN

Up and at 'Em

Bigfoot and Julia Gillian's father had returned by the time Julia Gillian made her way to the kitchen. Her mother was eating a bowl of oatmeal with butter and salt. Her mother was the only person Julia Gillian knew who put butter and salt on her oatmeal. Long ago, when she had pointed out that this was an odd habit, her mother had taken an extra-big bite of her oatmeal with butter and salt.

"So what?" she had said. "Shouldn't I be able to eat my oatmeal exactly the way I want?"

Julia Gillian's father was eating cinnamon raisin toast. He loved cinnamon raisin toast. He used so much cinnamon sugar that the entire surface of the toast turned dark. Her father had created his own cinnamon sugar recipe, and it contained three times the normal amount of cinnamon.

"Hi, Dad."

"Good morning, Julia Gillian."

Her father pointed to Bigfoot.

"I already took him out," he said. "You were sleeping so peacefully that I couldn't bear to disturb you."

Julia Gillian did not look at her mother, although she could feel her mother looking at her. Now she felt terrible. Here was her poor father, being so kind to his sleeping daughter. And she had lied outright. Should she confess? She did not know what to do.

"Dad?"

"Yes, Julia Gillian? Is anything on your mind?"

Now her father's eyes were wide, with a certain look in them. Suddenly Julia Gillian knew that her father knew she had only been pretending to sleep.

"I'm waiting," he said in a singsong way.

Julia Gillian had been caught red-handed, and the only thing to do was apologize in a sincere tone of voice and hope for the best.

"I'm sorry, Dad," said Julia Gillian.

"Apology accepted," said her father. "You do a very good impression of a sleeping child. Now, your mother and I have been considering your consequences."

In the Gillians' world, consequences was another word for punishment, although, as well-trained teachers, Julia Gillian's parents preferred not to use the word *punishment.* Julia Gillian did not enjoy being punished.

Usually her parents' consequences were mild — washing the living room windows or scrubbing the bathtub, for example, which were chores that all three of them disliked — but still, being punished was not a good thing.

"Yes, consequences," said her mother.

Her parents looked at each other. Julia Gillian saw them exchange a certain look and she knew that her consequence had already been decided. She had a sinking feeling.

"Dear, what about —"

"Yes, dear, what about —"

"Doing a little —"

Oh no. Julia Gillian knew what was coming, and here it came.

"— reading in your green book," said her father.

"Yes, the green book that you never finished," said her mother. "You know, the one on your bookshelf with the ponytail holders around it."

Julia Gillian looked down at Bigfoot, waiting so patiently beside her. He looked up with sympathy in his eyes and slowly wagged his tail.

"I don't like that book," said Julia Gillian.

"How do you know you don't like it if you haven't finished it?" said her mother.

"Yes, how do you know?" said her father.

"I just know."

"No, you don't," said her mother. "Not until you finish it."

"That's your consequence," said her father. "Fifteen minutes of green-book reading per day, until the book is done. Beginning this morning."

"But Bigfoot hasn't had his nine-square-block morning walk yet," Julia Gillian pointed out.

Bigfoot was a dog of routine, and Bigfoot was used to a nine-square-block morning walk, and Bigfoot had not been on his walk, now had he? Her parents could not argue with this logic.

"Go ahead and take him on his walk," said her father.

"Yes, go ahead," said her mother. "The green book will still be there upon your return."

CHAPTER TWELVE

Unfairness

Before she took Bigfoot out on his walk, Julia Gillian sat for a while on her bed, thinking about the wider world. Not much about it seemed fair this morning. For the tiny crime of pretending to be asleep, she was now being forced to read a book she hated.

Bigfoot seemed to know how much she dreaded her punishment. Once outside, he kept his eyes to the sidewalk and trotted along as though this walk were something that he must do, but did not want to do.

"It's not fair," said Julia Gillian to Bigfoot. "They just want to torture me."

Bigfoot raised his head a little, as if in agreement.

"What kind of parents force their child to read a book she's afraid of?"

Julia Gillian's parents did not, in actuality, know that she was afraid of the green book, but still. Bigfoot kept trudging. They were nearing Percy's house now, and she could hear him yapping in his yard. For a moment, she considered turning around. Percy had been ignoring Bigfoot for a year now, and maybe he always would. Was Julia Gillian causing her dog pain by continuing to walk him past Percy's house?

"Maybe we should go the other way today, Bigfoot," she said. "I've had just about enough of that little dog."

But Bigfoot could not resist. He tugged on the leash, and Julia Gillian decided that Bigfoot could make his

own decision about Percy. As they approached the yard, where Percy was digging a hole underneath his family's flowering crab apple tree — dirt flying everywhere — Bigfoot let out a small moan of longing. The lines of his body all pointed toward Percy. Julia Gillian knew that there was nothing Bigfoot would like more than to be in that yard, helping Percy dig his hole.

"Maybe you should give up, Bigfoot."

Percy might never be Bigfoot's friend, but Julia Gillian did not have the heart to say that to her dog. She kept a firm grip on the leash until they were safely around the corner. Once out of sight of Percy, Bigfoot relaxed and returned to the rhythm of the walk, leaving Julia Gillian free to think about the cruelty of her parents.

What about all the years that she had taken for granted that Bigfoot had been her babysitter? Wasn't that lie much worse than her own?

The longer she thought, the worse she felt. There was her parents' Bigfoot-as-babysitter lie, and there was their first-day-of-kindergarten lie. Julia Gillian began to think about her other woes, such as the meerkat in the claw machine. For three years, she had been trying to win that meerkat. For three years, she had chanted her mantra and predicted that this time, the meerkat would be hers. But three years was a long time. In fact, it was one third of Julia Gillian's life, and the meerkat was still stuck in the claw machine.

And what about the green book? She pictured that

green book, back home, waiting for her, bound with ponytail holders on her bookshelf.

"They want me to suffer," she said to her dog. "They're mean. Mean, mean, mean."

Julia Gillian knew that her parents were not mean, but sometimes it felt good to exaggerate. Bigfoot trotted steadily on, in the direction of Bryant Hardware, the bakery, and Lake Calhoun, while she thought about all the ways in which her parents were mean and the wider world unfair.

Bigfoot raised his head and pointed his nose at Bryant Hardware, which they were now passing. A new sign had been added: FALL BULBS HERE NEXT WEEK! The Bryant Hardware window, like Julia Gillian, was skilled in the art of knowing. And if fall bulbs were on their way, then the window knew that summer was coming to a close. School would be starting in a few weeks. That meant waiting at the corner for the school bus. That meant the heavy backpack, a green one this year, and a new teacher who would no doubt require lots of reading, a new classroom schedule, a new everything. Most important, it meant no more long morning walks with Bigfoot.

Fall bulbs were just one more thing that wasn't fair. Why couldn't anything stay the same?

Julia Gillian gave a little tug on the leash, so that Bigfoot would know they were not stopping at Bryant Hardware today. Today was Tuesday, not a claw machine day. Ordinarily Julia Gillian would be impatient to try again, but today she did not even care. The meerkat had been waiting for three long years. In such a long string of failures, one more day would make no difference.

"The world is so unfair, Bigfoot," said Julia Gillian.

This was true, and there was no sense hiding it, especially from Bigfoot, who always listened to her.

Her dog, who always pushed his nose into her legs and rubbed his head against her thigh. Her dog, who when she thought about it was really the only living being that truly cared about her. Bigfoot would never force her to read a book that scared her. Bigfoot would never force her to read any book at all. Why couldn't dogs rule the world?

CHAPTER THIRTEEN

Reading Very Slowly

Julia Gillian and Bigfoot did not stop at Bryant Hardware, or the bakery, or the DOGS! PLEASE HELP YOURSELVES! bowl. They marched around their nine-square-block circuit and then marched back home.

"How was your walk?" said her father when she walked into the living room.

Both her father and her mother were sitting at the dining room table. Julia Gillian had a flash of hope that they might have quit studying for the day and decided to take their daughter on a picnic to Lake Harriet Rose Garden, or perhaps even to the water park, but no.

"Good."

"Just in time for some reading," said her mother.

"Fifteen minutes," said her father.

"Do you want me to set the timer?"

Julia Gillian shook her head. She was nine years old, for heaven's sake. She was perfectly capable of marking off a fifteen-minute segment of time.

"Come on,

Bigfoot," said Julia Gillian to her dog, and they walked down the hall to her bedroom.

There was the green book, silent and deadly in its usual place on the highest shelf of the bookcase. The ponytail holders held tight, and Julia Gillian did not want to slip them off, but slip them off she did. From his long magenta pillow, Bigfoot gave her a sympathetic look and thumped his tail encouragingly.

"Well," said Julia Gillian, and she opened the book. "Here goes nothing."

Her sinking feeling of unhappy-ending-ahead returned. She glanced at her clock and made a mental note as to when she would be able to stop reading. Then she had a flash of inspiration. If she read extremely slowly, say one sentence per minute, she would barely be able to make it through a single page before her fifteen minutes were up. This was a brilliant idea, and Julia Gillian was impressed that she had thought it up.

"We left off on page thirty-seven, Bigfoot," she said. "At the part where the boy is hauling his dog into the tree house with that pulley-basket thing. Remember?"

Bigfoot thumped his tail.

Julia Gillian glanced at page thirty-seven and another excellent idea came to her. She would read the green book aloud to Bigfoot. That way she would have companionship through the darkness that lay ahead. And Bigfoot was a good companion. Indeed, Bigfoot was perhaps the best companion in the world.

"'The'," read Julia Gillian.

She glanced at her clock again. Reading *the* had taken approximately one second. It was imperative that Julia Gillian slow down if she was going to make one sentence last an entire minute. Bigfoot tilted his head and hung his pink tongue out in an appealing manner.

"'Booooooooooooooooy,'" she read.

She glanced at the clock again. Still too fast. This was not easy.

"'Began. To. Haul. His. Dog. Into. The. Tree. House.'"

Not even fifteen seconds had passed, and Julia Gillian was reading as slowly as it was possible for her or

any human being in the history of the world to read, and yet she was still not reading slowly enough. This was not good.

She looked at Bigfoot. The thought came to her that she would like to be a dog instead of a human child. Yes, she would like to be a dog, living with a little girl who loved her more than anything, a little girl who would take her on long walks every day to the bakery, to the hardware store, to the kind Girard Avenue house of DOGS! PLEASE HELP YOURSELVES! Now Julia Gillian felt like crying, because she would so much rather be a dog than a child. She would like to be a dog with a long magenta pillow, a dog who did not have cruel parents who forced their child to read green books that she was afraid to read.

"I'm not a dog," said Julia Gillian to Bigfoot. "That's the whole problem right there."

Bigfoot thumped his tail.

A minute had passed. Back to the green book. She decided to flip through some of the pages very quickly to see if she could pick out any individual words as the pages flashed by. There was no harm in doing that. It was still reading, wasn't it? An unusual form of reading, but still, reading was reading.

Flip.

The pages flashed by and Julia Gillian concentrated on the words as they went zipping past her eyes.

Boy.

Tree.

Fall.

Old.

Broken.

Dog.

"No," said Julia Gillian.

She immediately shut the green book and strung the ponytail holders around it again. Instead of putting the green book back on the highest shelf of the bookcase, she opened her screen window and placed the green book on her fire escape. Then she shut the screen window and the glass window and locked it. She looked through the glass at the green book lying on the slats of the iron fire escape.

"Good-bye," said Julia Gillian to the green book. "I hope I never see you again."

The window was shut, and the bound book was alone on the fire escape, but still, the words that Julia Gillian had read as they flashed by were stuck in her head. She would never be able to get them out.

Broken. Old. Dog.

Julia Gillian tried to put them together in a different order.

Old broken dog. Dog broken old. Broken dog old.

Nothing worked. No matter how she rearranged the words, there was a dog, and the dog was old and broken.

CHAPTER FOURTEEN

Something Needs to Be Said

With the green book bound and alone on the fire escape, Julia Gillian went straight to her mask box. She plucked out her wolf mask, which was a fairly new mask that she had not yet worn in public, and put it on, and then she went into the dining room.

"A wolf mask," said her father, looking up from a large brown book with a title that was so long it took up three lines. "Very nice."

"Wow," said her mother. "I didn't know you knew how to make a wolf mask."

"It's a balloon and papier-mâché mask," said Julia Gillian.

"So it is," agreed her father.

Julia Gillian stood before her parents. She needed to say something to them, but she was not sure how to say it.

"How did the reading go?" said her mother.

Julia Gillian made a face, but since she was wearing her wolf mask, the face she made was not visible to

her parents. She said nothing. Her parents exchanged a look.

"Is there something you want to tell us, Julia Gillian?" said her father.

"Yes, Father."

Julia Gillian heard herself saying "Father" instead of "Dad." The wish to be a girl living long ago, a girl in a velvet dress with a father who smoked a pipe by the fire, came over her. She felt sure that back in those long ago days, there had been no such thing as global warming. Back then, teachers didn't have to take double summer-school course loads in order to become the best teachers in the history of the world. Back then, the green book had not even been written.

"Yes, Father, there is," she said again.

She waited. So did they. Her parents were patient people, and Julia Gillian knew from experience that this waiting could go on a long time.

"It's unfair," she said.

"What's unfair?" said her mother.

"Everything."

Her parents looked at each other and then back at their daughter.

"Why do you read that newspaper every day?" said Julia Gillian.

She had not known she was going to say that, but there it was. Her parents looked at each other again.

"Because we like to know what's going on in the wider world," said her father. "That's why we read the newspaper every day."

Behind her wolf mask, Julia Gillian rolled her eyes. How tired she was of hearing those words. It was useless to try talking with her parents about the wider world. Beside her, Bigfoot angled his head upward and met her eyes. He thumped his tail definitively. Julia Gillian felt the need to do something decisive, something out of the ordinary, something that would show her parents that she meant business.

"Come on, Bigfoot," said Julia Gillian. "We're going to the kitchen."

Julia Gillian pushed the wolf mask back on her head and opened the freezer. There sat the box of Popsicles. The freezer air rushed out at her as if it were happy to be freed from the cold. The kitchen window was open,

unlike her bedroom window, which was now closed in order to keep out the green book. It was possible that Julia Gillian's window would remain closed for the rest of her life.

"What are you doing, Daughter?" her father called from the dining room.

"Getting a Popsicle," she called back.

She was not allowed to eat a Popsicle unless her parents said she could, on account of the sugar factor. That was how her parents termed it: the sugar factor. Sugar was not good for a person, her parents said. Julia Gillian disagreed, because sugar was one of the tastiest treats in the world, and how could something that tasty not be a good thing?

"A sour apple Popsicle," she called.

She added that detail to emphasize to her parents — who were silent — that she was going to eat her Popsicle whether they liked it or not. If her parents were going to make her read a book with an unhappy ending, then why should Julia Gillian not be able to get herself a Popsicle without asking permission? She was nine years old now. Surely a nine-year-old could decide for herself when a Popsicle was appropriate and when it was not.

"Would you like one, Dad?" she called to the still-silent dining room. "How about you, Mom?"

She was truly overstepping her parameters with that question, but she asked it anyway.

"Because there's plenty more where this one came from," sang Julia Gillian in a carefree sort of voice.

She peeled the wrapper off the Popsicle, making sure

that she did so as loudly as possible. If her parents came into the kitchen with their arms crossed and that certain look on their faces, she would look right back at them.

Silence from the dining room.

Julia Gillian swiped her tongue down the sour apple Popsicle. Yikes. It certainly was sour.

"This sour apple Popsicle is really tasty," she called. "Are you sure you don't want one?"

"Julia," said her mother. "Please come into the dining room."

Julia, but no Gillian. The sour apple Popsicle was beginning to melt in the heat, small drops gathering at the bottom edge of the wooden stick. She licked off the drops and made a face at the sourness. She did not even want this Popsicle, not really, and now her mother had left off the Gillian half of Julia Gillian, and that meant even more consequences.

"Come on, Bigfoot," she said.

On the way to the dining room, she placed one foot exactly in front of the other. That way, if a woodland tracker decided to trace her footsteps, he would be amazed at the precision of her steps. She held her Popsicle before her like a spear and concentrated. Placing one foot exactly in front of the other was harder than it seemed. Beside her, Bigfoot glanced up and tilted his head.

Drip. Drip.

The Popsicle was dripping onto Julia Gillian's precisely placed feet. She quickly licked it to catch the melting drops, but the drops kept falling. Once in the dining room, she stood before her parents, holding her dripping Popsicle spear. It was a nasty, sour Popsicle, and she had not even wanted it to begin with, but she felt that her parents had forced her into it, with their green-book consequences and their unhappy newspaper with its wider world. *Global warming. War. Budget cuts.*

The time had come to say something, and it was up to Julia Gillian to say it.

"I hate that green book," she said.

"Why?" said her father.

"Because. The boy's dog is old. He's an *old* dog."

Her parents looked at each other.

"Bigfoot's getting older, you know," said Julia Gillian. "He's nine."

Her parents tilted their heads and looked at her in a way similar to the way Bigfoot looked at her.

"Someday Bigfoot will be *old*," said Julia Gillian.

It was a sunny day and the sunshine coming in through the window by the fireplace brought out little flickers in her mother's hair.

"And broken," said Julia Gillian.

Her parents did not say anything. They kept looking at her, and her Popsicle kept dripping, and Bigfoot stood staunchly by her side.

"Think about it," said Julia Gillian.

CHAPTER FIFTEEN

Is It Better to Know?

KNOCK. KNOCK. KNOCK.

KnockKnockKnock.

Knock. Knock. Knock.

Enzo was lying in her indoor reading hammock. In the fierce heat she was spending much of her time reading, and she had gradually moved more and more *accoutrements*, which was a French word meaning "things," into the hammock with her. Flat and fluffy pillows of all shapes and sizes surrounded her, along with assorted beverages in spill-proof bottles. Extra socks should her feet become cold as she read, which was something that tended to happen to Enzo even in the middle of a heat wave. Next to the hammock a folding tray was set up, on which rested several bowls and plates of food. Enzo's indoor reading hammock was becoming a home within a home.

"You've got to try some of these Zap creations," said Enzo. "He's been on a baking binge lately."

"Anything good?"

"That depends on your taste," said Enzo, and pointed at an orange bowl. "Do you like blue food?"

Julia Gillian peered into the bowl. The contents were definitely blue.

"I thought not," said Enzo. "I don't either. But you came down here for a reason, didn't you, Noodlie?"

Enzo could always tell when Julia Gillian came down for a reason. She was quick that way. And now she was calling Julia Gillian by her favorite nickname, Noodlie, which made her feel both weak and relieved at the same time.

"I came down here to talk about the green book," she said.

"Then let's talk about it," said Enzo, and she sat up as straight as was possible in her indoor reading hammock. She was all business. "Where is the green book right now?"

"Well, I wrapped my ponytail holders around it. So it's shut tight. And I put it out on my fire escape."

Enzo narrowed her eyes and frowned.

"Did you close your window?"

"Yes."

"But, Noodlie, aren't you hot?"

"Yes. I am."

Enzo nodded. Julia Gillian sat in the chair by Enzo's hammock and waited. Enzo had all the facts: The green book was shut tight and banished to the fire escape, subject to the wind and rain and sun and sleet. Enzo would know what to do now. She was that kind of girl.

"Well," said Enzo. "You have to ask yourself this: Is it better to know the possibly unhappy ending and have it settled, or is it better never to know at all?"

Julia Gillian considered Enzo's question. If she read the green book all the way through, it was probable that she would be very sad. Although she didn't know this for certain, she was rarely wrong when it came to the art of knowing. If she did not ever finish the green book, she might possibly avoid feeling sad about the ending.

"It boils down to this, Noodlie," said Enzo. "Are you going to risk an unhappy ending, or are you going to live in fear?"

Without moving from her hammock, Enzo reached over to the tray of Zap creations, plucked a yellow chiplike wafer from one of the bowls, and popped it into her mouth. She chewed thoughtfully and gazed at Julia Gillian.

"I'm going to live in fear," said Julia Gillian.

"Okay then," said Enzo.

She opened her *Collected Plays of William Shakespeare* and returned to her reading. It was not in Enzo's nature to question Julia Gillian's decisions.

✿

Back in her room, Julia Gillian sat on her bed. Her stuffed whistling marmot was wedged between the wall and the bed, and she extracted him. Bigfoot watched closely. While Bigfoot was not exactly jealous of her stuffed whistling marmot, he did pay close attention whenever she held it.

Julia Gillian retrieved her winter quilt from the top shelf in her closet and placed it in front of her closed window, and then she placed one of her pillows on top of the quilt. She set her stuffed whistling marmot on top of the quilt and pillow. Now she had a quilt-pillow-whistling-marmot tower. When she lay down on her bed, she could no longer see what waited for her out on the fire escape.

"Good-bye, green book," said Julia Gillian. She made up a little spontaneous song of good-bye.

Good-bye, green bookishness,
alone out there on the fire escape
where you have no friends.
Enjoy the sun and the rain
and the sleet and the snow.

Julia Gillian sang her new song several times, avoiding looking anywhere near the window. Her favorite line was *Good-bye, green bookishness.*

Julia Gillian patted her bed so that Bigfoot would jump up next to her. *Jump* was not exactly the right word, because Bigfoot was so large. *Haul* was a better word.

"Haul yourself up here," she said to Bigfoot.

Bigfoot rose wearily from his long magenta pillow. He placed both paws on Julia Gillian's bed and made a valiant effort.

"Come on now," said Julia Gillian. "I don't have a pulley-basket thing to help you out. You'll have to put some muscle into it."

Bigfoot tried again. This time he made it. He flopped next to Julia Gillian and laid his head in her lap. Julia Gillian wished she had not mentioned the pulley basket, because that reminded her of the green book. She decided to sing her song of green bookishness again.

"Well, Bigfoot," she said to her dog. "I guess we'll be living in fear for the rest of our lives."

Bigfoot tried to thump his tail, but the quilt-pillow-whistling-marmot tower was in his way, and the best he could manage was a half wag.

CHAPTER SIXTEEN
A Life of Fear

Living in fear made it difficult for Julia Gillian to get a good night's rest. She had to make sure that her quilt-pillow-whistling-marmot tower was intact, so that if she woke up in the middle of the night she would not accidentally look out her window at the fire escape and see the green book outlined in the light of the street lamp.

And in the morning, she had to feel around with her fingers to make sure that the quilt-pillow-whistling-marmot tower was still there and still blocking the view of the fire escape.

It was also important that she not have dreams that

would cause her to move and possibly disturb the tower. It was hard not to dream, and if truth be told, dreaming was something that Julia Gillian had always enjoyed. She had often dreamed about winning the meerkat in the claw machine, and that dream had been a wonderful dream. But no longer. If she dreamed, Julia Gillian might turn over. She might kick. She might even thrash. And then the tower would come tumbling down.

Might she have to give up dreaming entirely?

If so, how could she train herself into not dreaming?

What's more, it was not only the green book itself that was scary now. The fire escape, the window, and even the quilt-pillow-whistling-marmot tower had taken on a feeling of danger and fright. This was sad, because Julia Gillian had always loved her fire escape. She had loved sitting on her bed and looking out her window down through the fire escape, seeing what was happening down below on the street, who might be walking by, if there were any interesting dogs out on walks.

Now Julia Gillian could not even look in the general direction of the fire escape without feeling afraid and a bit panicky. She would never have predicted that she would feel this way about her fire escape. But that was the way of the wider world. Everything changed, even if you didn't want it to change.

By Thursday morning, Julia Gillian was exhausted. She lay in bed with her eyes closed, considering the various facts of her new green-book-avoiding existence. Then she felt about with her hands to make sure that the quilt-pillow-whistling-marmot tower was still intact. The whistling marmot seemed to be slipping off the top, and she readjusted it as best she could with her eyes closed. Was this what it was like to be blind?

She opened her eyes and avoided looking anywhere near the window. She looked instead in the direction of her dog, lying on his long magenta pillow patiently waiting for her to open her eyes.

Living in fear isn't easy.

That was the thought that Julia Gillian beamed telepathically to Bigfoot, who thumped his tail in sympathy.

K N O C K. K N O C K. K N O C K.

KnockKnockKnock.

Knock. Knock. Knock.

Julia Gillian kept her fist in the air, ready to knock the secret code again if Enzo did not answer. She looked down at the neat row of Enzo-Zap shoes, lined up in the hallway. *Just this once*, she thought, and she slipped her feet into Zap's brown lace-ups. Bigfoot bent his head to her feet and sniffed.

"Noodlie?" called Enzo. "Come on in."

Julia Gillian opened the door with her key. There was Enzo, lying in her indoor reading hammock, surrounded with her pillows of all shapes and sizes, her giant book of Shakespeare, and her extra socks. And there was Zap, sitting at the table eating a not-blue something that resembled a croissant, full of butter and air.

"Hey, JG," said Zap.

He waved the buttery airy thing in the air.

"Want a croissant-thingy? I invented it myself."

"Croissants were invented in France, Zap," said Enzo. "Don't pretend you're smarter than you are."

Julia Gillian stroked Bigfoot's head. Zap and Enzo zipped insults back and forth at each other but they were always smiling, and even though they were brother and sister and many brothers and sisters did not get along, Enzo and Zap did. They completely loved each other. What would it be like to live with Enzo and Zap? Julia Gillian was quite sure that they did not read the unhappy newspaper every morning, and neither of them was taking a double course load of summer school classes.

"Come in, Noodlie," said Enzo. She lay her giant book of Shakespeare on her lap. "Come in and stay awhile, and bring your large dog with you."

They stepped inside, and Julia Gillian closed the door. Enzo glanced at Julia Gillian's feet.

"Nice shoes."

"Yeah, nice shoes," said Zap.

Oh dear. Julia Gillian had forgotten to take off Zap's shoes. She considered backing out of the apartment, removing the shoes, and re-entering in her orange sandals, but it was too late.

"I just put them on for luck," she said, and the minute she said that she realized that it was true.

Zap nodded.

"No problem, JG."

That was the thing about Zap and Enzo. They did not question. They merely accepted. Julia Gillian felt a surge of happiness to be in their apartment with them,

Zap strewing croissant-thingy crumbs on the table, Enzo rocking gently in her indoor reading hammock, one toe on the floor pushing her back and forth.

"Hey, JG," said Zap. "You mastered the claw yet?"

He moved his hands up and down as if he were weighing the air, but Julia Gillian knew that he was miming the act of juggling. Zap had been waiting patiently for years to teach her the art of juggling. While Julia Gillian did want to add the Art of Juggling to her list of accomplishments, she knew that day was still a long way off. It occurred to her that it had been quite a while since she had heaved up the corner of her mattress and extracted her list. It seemed to be getting harder to master the things she wanted to master. Was this, too, something that happened when you got older?

"No."

"Still working on that meerkat?"

Julia Gillian nodded. The thought of just how long she had been trying to win the meerkat made her feel tired and slow. She pictured the worried little girl from yesterday, sitting on her front stoop with her untied shoes by her side. It was beginning to seem that no matter who you were, life truly was not easy.

"Well, all things in good time," said Zap. "To the bakery I go."

He danced his way to the door, singing a little song — "*Good-bye to you, little sister, and good-bye to you, JG*" — and bowed to them both. Making up little songs and dances on the spot was the sort of thing Zap did. Julia Gillian thought of the little song she herself

2A

had made up, her song of green bookishness, and for a moment she felt happy that she and Zap were alike in this way.

"So what's up, Noodlie?" said Enzo when the door had closed behind Zap.

Julia Gillian looked down at her feet inside Zap's enormous shoes. If Zap's shoes were a dog, they would be a dog the size of Bigfoot.

"I think I made a mistake," she said.

"Are we talking about a certain green book?"

"Yes."

"What about this certain green book?"

Julia Gillian paused. She wanted to tell Enzo about the quilt-pillow-whistling-marmot tower in front of her window, but she was a little embarrassed. Enzo narrowed her eyes and waited. Enzo was the kind of person who would sit and wait, as long as it took.

"There's sort of a pile in front of my window now," said Julia Gillian.

"A pile?"

"Of things. You sort of can't see out the window anymore."

Enzo nodded. Now she had the information that she needed.

"Well, Noodlie," she said. "Sometimes the only way out is through."

That was something that Enzo was fond of saying. It meant that sometimes you needed to be brave and do whatever it was you were afraid of doing. Julia Gillian hated it when Enzo said these words. She looked at Bigfoot and sighed. She tugged gently on one of his ears. Bigfoot tilted his head and gazed at her in sympathy.

"Bye, Enzo," said Julia Gillian.

"Courage," said Enzo.

CHAPTER SEVENTEEN

The Time Has Come

Julia Gillian moved her quilt-pillow-whistling-marmot tower to one side and unlocked her window. She slid it up, and she slid up the screen window as well. Then she climbed out onto the fire escape. Bigfoot did not like the fire escape, but if the fire escape was where Julia Gillian wanted to be, then he would put up with it, because that was the kind of dog he was. He moaned a tiny moan and then clambered out the window after her.

The bound green book was hot to the touch. It had been sitting in the sun all day and it had soaked up all of that sun warmth. Julia Gillian sighed. She removed the ponytail holders, first the yellow and then the blue. She put them around her wrist for safekeeping. That way, in case she felt the need for a ponytail or two later, she would be all set.

"Here goes nothing," said Julia Gillian to Bigfoot.

She sat down in the corner of the fire escape, so that she could lean against the iron bars. Bigfoot lay down next to her.

Before she opened the green book to the bookmarked page, she looked up. Through the fire escape slats above her, she could see the flowers in Mr. Hoffbeck's window box. Mr. Hoffbeck took excellent care of his flowers. Sometimes, before the days of the quilt-pillow-whistling-marmot tower, Julia Gillian had woken up to see sparkling drops falling past her window in the first rays of the sun. That was Mr. Hoffbeck, watering his flowers.

"Yes, here we go," said Julia Gillian to Bigfoot.

She was trying to get up her courage. *The only way out is through,* Enzo had said. The slats of the fire escape were warm underneath Julia Gillian's legs. She briefly considered taking a nap right there, with Bigfoot next to her. But what if, in her sleep, she had a bad dream — a dream about an old broken dog, say — and she tumbled down all four flights of the fire escape and injured her head so that she was unable to read for the rest of her livelong days? Then she would not be able to get through the green book even if she wanted to, and she would truly have to live in fear for the rest of her life.

"Let's just get it over with," she said to Bigfoot.

Bigfoot opened one eye and gazed at her. He tried to thump his tail, but because he was on the fire escape, his tail brushed right between two of the slats. This was one of the reasons why Bigfoot did not like the fire escape. He pulled his tail back up and moaned again ever so slightly.

"Let's see, where did we leave off?" said Julia Gillian.

Julia Gillian knew exactly where she had left off, but she was stalling. She opened the book to page thirty-seven.

"Oh yes," she said. "Right here is where we left off. Right at the broken old dog."

Bigfoot closed his one open eye. Julia Gillian began to read.

CHAPTER EIGHTEEN

The Unhappy Words

KNOCK. KNOCK. KNOCK.

KnockKnockKnock.

Knock. Knock. Knock.

Enzo was sitting at the dining table eating her lunch, which was a bowl of noodles with an unusual-looking sauce. Enzo waved her chopsticks in the air. If at all possible, Enzo preferred to eat with chopsticks. She said it made the food taste more interesting. Seeing the chopsticks made Julia Gillian think of the Quang Vietnamese Restaurant. How she wished she were at the Quang on a Saturday night, sitting in her favorite corner booth, waiting for her egg rolls and strawberry bubble tea to arrive. Enzo pointed her chopsticks at the bowl of noodles.

"Help yourself," she said. "It's a Zap creation, but it's really good. Extra chopsticks in the silverware drawer."

Julia Gillian shook her head. She felt too tired to speak, so she beamed a thought telepathically toward Enzo: *No, thank you*, and Enzo nodded.

"Well?" said Enzo. "Mission accomplished?"

Julia Gillian shrugged.

"Did it end the way you thought it would?" said Enzo.

Julia Gillian nodded.

"Not going to talk?"

Julia Gillian shook her head.

"That bad, then?"

Julia Gillian nodded.

"I figured it might be," said Enzo. "I'm sorry, Noodlie."

Julia Gillian wove her fingers through the fur on Bigfoot's neck and tugged slightly. Bigfoot lowered his head and rubbed his cheek against her leg. There was nothing else to say, so she turned to go, and Bigfoot followed her.

"I finished the green book," said Julia Gillian to her parents.

Her mother and father looked up from the dining table, where they had sat all day long, reading their many heavy books and taking breaks to quiz each other. They were drinking coffee, which they sometimes did in the late afternoon if they were very tired. They looked tired, and their eyes were rimmed with red. What was the point of becoming the best teachers in the history of the world if it made your eyes red and you couldn't go to the water park or on picnics to the Lake Harriet Rose Garden?

"Good job, honey," said her father.

"Yes, good job," said her mother. "See, that wasn't so bad, now was it?"

They turned back to their books. There they sat, surrounded with coffee and quizzes and books upon books, and they did not even care that Julia Gillian had finished her green book. It did not seem to bother them that some endings were unhappy, too unhappy to bear.

"You know something?" said Julia Gillian.

"What?" said her father.

"The dog died."

It hurt to say those words. But they had to be said.

"I'm sorry," said her father.

"So am I," said her mother.

They did look sorry. But they were not the ones who had to read the green book, were they? They were not the ones who had to watch as the boy put his arms around his old dog and held him until he took his last breath. The worst of it was that the old dog in the green book had not been old in human years. The green-book dog had been ten, just one year older than Bigfoot. Sometimes the only way out was through, but Julia Gillian had gone through, and she did not yet feel as if she were out.

✿

It was time to make a new mask, and Julia Gillian knew exactly the kind of mask it was time to make.

"First," she said to Bigfoot, "we need to gather our supplies."

She opened the back door of their apartment and Bigfoot followed her into the darkened landing, where the Gillians kept their cans and bottles and plastic and newspaper for the large green and white recycling truck, which came every other Tuesday.

Three brown grocery bags were filled — stuffed, actually — with discarded newspapers.

"These people read way too many newspapers," said Julia Gillian, who, when she was annoyed with them, sometimes referred to her parents as "these people."

She went through each bag and pulled out the front page sections and stacked them in a neat pile. There they were, the unhappy words that caused the shaking heads, the clucks of the tongue, gathered together in all the little print in all the little stories, for all the world to see.

Bigfoot observed while Julia Gillian cut certain parts of the front page sections into thin strips with the black-handled scissors that were kept in the pen cup in the kitchen. Then she mixed up the flour and water in her special papier-mâché-mixing bowl. Usually she made animal masks, but not today.

"Well, Bigfoot," she said. "Let's get going."

Bigfoot thumped his tail on the floor. It was nice to have a mask-making companion. Julia Gillian tipped her head sideways the way that Bigfoot did, and then she went to work.

CHAPTER NINETEEN

Time to Take Action

It was Friday morning. Julia Gillian woke up to the sun shining through her window, which was no longer obscured by the quilt-pillow-whistling-marmot tower. She had opened her window when she went to bed, and now, in the early morning, a fresh breeze blew through the screen. The quilt-pillow-whistling-marmot tower had meant not only living in fear, but also living in a hot, stuffy room. Bigfoot looked up from his long magenta pillow, where he had been patiently waiting for her to open her eyes, and thumped his tail. He was such an agreeable dog. The dog in the green book had been agreeable, too, but it was no use thinking about that now.

"Today is a meerkat day, Bigfoot," said Julia Gillian. "I feel it in my bones."

The new mask had dried overnight. Julia Gillian stapled a shoelace onto it and then put it on. The mask was a good fit: not too big and not too tight. Then she walked to the kitchen, where her parents sat with their unhappy newspaper.

"Hello," she said, through the fresh scent of newly dry papier-mâché.

She inclined her head first to her mother, and then to her father, as if she were a mask model and they were her audience. Her parents tilted their heads at her in puzzlement.

"That's a new one, isn't it?" said her father.

"Indeed it is," said Julia Gillian.

"Do you have a name for this one?" said her mother.

"Indeed I do," said Julia Gillian. "This mask is called the Mask of Unhappy Newspaperness."

She took the new mask off her head and hung it from the lamp that dangled above the table, where it twisted gently this way and that. Some of the pasted-on words were big and black — ***global warming, budget cuts, skyrocketing costs of health insurance, war*** —

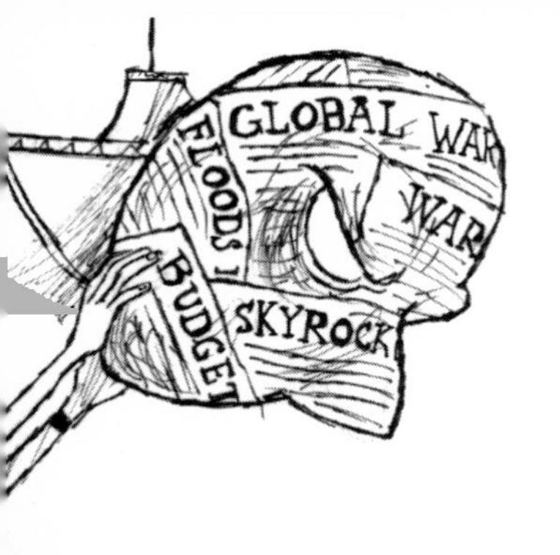

and her parents squinted, the better to read them.

"Come, Bigfoot," said Julia Gillian.

Her father took his eyes from the new mask and opened his mouth. Julia Gillian could tell that he was about to ask where she and Bigfoot were going, and she held up her hand.

"We're going to Bryant Hardware," she said. "And we'll be back in an hour."

Her father closed his mouth. He exchanged a look with her mother. Then they both tilted their heads and peered again at the new mask, with its big black headlines, dangling before them.

On the way to Bryant Hardware, Bigfoot and Julia Gillian walked past Percy's house. No sign of Percy in the yard, but as they turned the corner, Julia Gillian saw his head appear in the window. Percy's barking was muffled through the glass, but still, there he was, yapping away as obnoxiously as ever. Bigfoot gazed mournfully in Percy's direction. This made Julia Gillian, who was already sad, even sadder. Why did life seem so hard these days?

When they reached Bryant Hardware, Julia Gillian and Bigfoot stood in front of the big display window. Just three days before, they had studied the display carefully, and while it was doubtful that anything would have changed since then, Julia Gillian liked to stay on top of things.

"See anything new, Bigfoot?"

Bigfoot tilted his head and wagged his tail. The summer water toys were still there, as were the grass seed and fertilizer. There was a surprise, though, one she hadn't expected. In the far corner hung a rake and a small tower of leaf bags. Julia Gillian shook her head.

"Leaf bags already," she said to Bigfoot.

The presence of the rake and leaf bags meant that summer was officially at its end. Soon the air would be crisp and cool. Soon leaf bags would appear before all the houses and apartment buildings of the city. Some of the leaf bags would be plain black, and some would be bright orange with grinning pumpkin faces. Soon it would be time for Julia Gillian to begin work on her annual Halloween mask.

✿

"No mask today, I see," said Mr. Bryant Senior.

"Not today," said Julia Gillian grimly.

Mr. Bryant Senior looked at her carefully.

"A girl on a mission, are you?"

"Yes."

Mr. Bryant Senior was exactly right. Julia Gillian was a girl on a mission, and she could feel in her bones that today was going to be a meerkat day.

"I finished my green book, Mr. Bryant Senior," she said.

She did not expect to hear herself saying those words, but there they were.

"That is quite an accomplishment," said Mr. Bryant Senior.

"Yes, it is."

Without going through the usual game of pretend, Mr. Bryant Senior placed two quarters in her hand. Julia Gillian and Bigfoot made their way past the lightbulbs and hose nozzles, straight to the claw machine. She pushed her quarters into the slots with a definitive shove.

Did Julia Gillian pause to chant her meerkat prayer? She did not.

Did she pause to close her eyes and visualize the claw coming straight down on the meerkat's head? She did not.

Beside her, Bigfoot was quiet and still. In the background, up by the cash register, Julia Gillian could hear the murmurings of Mr. Bryant Senior and a customer, but she could not hear what they were saying, and she did not care.

The claw machine sprang to life. The claw swung into action and sailed from its resting place in the corner straight to the pile of stuffed animals. The meerkat gazed at Julia Gillian with his dark eyes, and she gazed back. Just at the right moment, she pushed the button and lowered the claw over the meerkat's head. Down it went, with a serious and determined motion. And then it closed, right over the head of a —

skinny

brown

bat.

"Wait —" said Julia Gillian.

The claw gripped the bat around its neck and sailed it through the air to the exit chute.

"But —" said Julia Gillian.

The claw opened directly above the exit chute and dropped the bat straight into the black hole.

"Wait —" said Julia Gillian again.

Clunk.

Julia Gillian peered into the exit tray. The skinny bat gazed up at her with tiny brown eyes. Its mouth was partly open, revealing little pointed teeth. Its wings were spread as if it had been captured in midflight. It was an extremely realistic stuffed bat.

"Oh no," said Julia Gillian.

She could not believe what had just happened. The whole experience seemed like a dream: the march to the claw machine, the insertion of the quarters, the determined motion of the claw, the seizing of the bat.

"I don't want this bat," said Julia Gillian.

Bigfoot, next to her, stretched his neck up so that he too could peer into the exit tray. He wagged his tail and looked up at Julia Gillian hopefully.

"I want my meerkat," said Julia Gillian.

And there it was, her meerkat, still sitting atop the pile of stuffed animals. Julia Gillian felt as if time had slowed down, and she was all the Julia Gillians she had ever been, standing in this familiar spot, gazing into this familiar claw machine. *Meerkat meerkat, come to me.* But her meerkat had not come to her.

CHAPTER TWENTY

Home Again, and Quickly

"Goodness gracious, do we have a winner?"

Julia Gillian turned to see Mr. Bryant Senior and Mr. Bryant Junior standing behind her. They were smiling and clapping.

"No," said Julia Gillian. "We don't. I wanted the meerkat, and I got the bat."

"Bats are wonderful creatures," said Mr. Bryant Junior.

"That's true," said Mr. Bryant Senior.

"They eat more than half their weight in bugs every single night," said Mr. Bryant Junior.

"And you can't say that about a meerkat," said Mr. Bryant Senior. "Now can you?"

TOY PARADE

Julia Gillian did not care about what you could or could not say about a meerkat. She plucked the bat from the exit tray and held it between her thumb and forefinger.

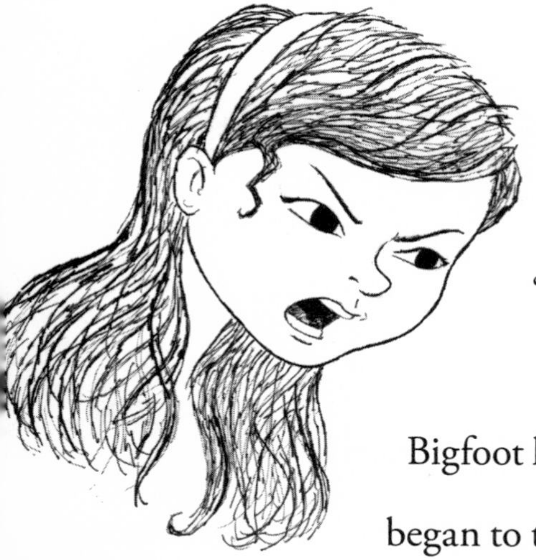

"Come on, Bigfoot," she said. "We're going straight home."

Out the door they marched. Bigfoot looked down at the sidewalk and began to trot. He always knew when Julia Gillian meant business. Julia Gillian held the leash in one hand and the bat in the other. The bat was scrawny and a bit ratty-looking. Its brown fur was not plush like the meerkat's fur, and its eyes had a shifty look.

"Look at this beady-eyed little thing," she said.

She held the bat out to Bigfoot and shook it

slightly. The bat's large ears wiggled in Bigfoot's face. He stopped walking.

"What is it, Bigfoot? Are you scared? It's creepy, I know."

Bigfoot extended his head, with his ears pulled back and his eyes narrowed, and he sniffed the bat. Julia Gillian shook the bat again and watched its large ears tremble. Just then, Bigfoot opened his mouth and closed his jaws around the bat. In her surprise, Julia Gillian let go, and Bigfoot, bat in mouth, shook his head happily.

"Bigfoot!" said Julia Gillian. "Drop that nasty bat this instant!"

Bigfoot began to walk again, faster this time. Julia Gillian pulled on the leash, but the fact was that Bigfoot weighed twice as much as she did, and when he wanted to walk, there was not much that Julia Gillian could do about it. She put on her pretend-grownup voice and hauled on the leash with all her strength.

"Stop, Bigfoot."

They were moving along at a good clip. Bigfoot showed no sign of stopping. Julia Gillian decided to pretend she was a grownup with a British accent. Maybe that would surprise him into slowing down.

"I say, Bigfoot, old chap. Halt at once."

Bigfoot kept trotting. There was nothing Julia Gillian could do, so she walked very fast. That way, it would look to everyone as if she was the one in charge, and Bigfoot was just trying to keep up with her. Julia Gillian made sure to nod and smile at everyone they passed. Now they were coming up on the worried little girl's house. There she was, out on her front steps again, shoes beside her, shoelaces dangling.

"Hello," said Julia Gillian. She waved and smiled.

The worried little girl looked up. The hopeless expression on her face changed to one of interest.

"Why are you walking so fast?"

"Exercise," said Julia Gillian, smiling brightly. "Good for you."

Bigfoot did not even look at the worried little girl. He trotted on, bat in mouth, bat ears swinging in time with his own larger ears. They were past the little girl now, but Julia Gillian turned around.

"No worries, matey," she called back. "You'll learn how to tie those shoes. G'day now."

Julia Gillian was walking so fast that her accents were jumbling up. Without thinking, her pretend-British accent had changed to a pretend-Australian accent. What next? This day was already terribly discombobulated.

Bigfoot and Julia Gillian flew along the sidewalk.

Julia Gillian wished that she was wearing her raccoon mask.

Bigfoot sped up. Julia Gillian broke into a trot. Did whistling marmots and bats get along? Whistling marmots lived in holes in the ground, from which they popped up every now and then to whistle at one another. Bats were creatures of the night, emerging under cover of darkness to gobble up more than half their weight in insects.

Bigfoot, Julia Gillian, and the stuffed bat turned the corner onto their block. The white picket fence of Percy's house flashed by. Julia Gillian tried to count the pickets — one, two, three, four five sixseveneightnine — but she felt a bit dizzy after five. Not to mention that in this heat, her T-shirt and shorts were wet with sweat. Bigfoot seemed not even to notice, although he usually moved as little as possible in this kind of heat.

Snobby little Percy zipped along the fence and yapped at Bigfoot. There. Surely that would slow Bigfoot down. But no. Not today. Today, Bigfoot was a dog on a mission.

And then they were there, at the double front doors of their own apartment building. Bigfoot stopped, his sides heaving. The bat fell from his mouth and his long pink tongue lolled out.

"Finally," said Julia Gillian.

She was having trouble catching her breath. The stuffed bat lay on the sidewalk, scrawny and damp, ears flattened on the pavement, beady eyes staring straight up. Truly, it was a repulsive little thing. Julia Gillian still could not believe that she had finally won at the claw machine, but she had not won her meerkat. Did this win still count as a win? She bent down to pick up the bat. She extended her thumb and forefinger.

Snap.

"Bigfoot!" said Julia Gillian.

Who could have known that Bigfoot could move so fast? He dipped his large head down to the sidewalk and, poof, the bat was back in his mouth. Julia Gillian looked down at him. For three years she had been trying to win a meerkat, and now she had won a bat. She did not want the bat, but it appeared that her dog was entranced with it. What an odd turn of events.

CHAPTER TWENTY-ONE

The Dark Lady

KNOCK. KNOCK. KNOCK.

KnockKnockKnock.

Knock. Knock. Knock.

"Come on in, Noodlie," called Enzo from within.

Julia Gillian unlocked the door and pushed it open. She was not yet ready to return upstairs to her own apartment, where the new mask hung from the kitchen light, and where her parents would look with surprise and interest at the lean brown bat dangling from Bigfoot's jaws. She nudged Bigfoot and together the three of them — Julia Gillian, Bigfoot, and the bat — squeezed through Enzo's door.

"What have we here?" said Enzo.

"We have me," said Julia Gillian. "Me and this bat."

Julia Gillian pointed at the stuffed bat drooping from Bigfoot's mouth.

"I can hardly believe it," said Enzo. "You're a winner!"

"No, I'm not. If I was a winner, I'd have the meerkat."

"Well," said Enzo. "Maybe Bigfoot's the winner."

"You don't get it," said Julia Gillian. "You don't understand."

Enzo obviously had no idea how Julia Gillian longed for that meerkat. It had been years of trying. Years! On top of the sad ending of the green book and the unhappy words in the unhappy newspaper and the parents who spent all their time studying, now she was looking at an undernourished beady-eyed bat instead of the plump and plush meerkat. Everything was wrong and nothing was right.

"Poodle, are you scowling?" said Enzo.

And now Enzo had called her "Poodle," the nickname she reserved for tension and displeasure. Indeed Julia Gillian was scowling. She focused her scowling on the bat, which was the worst stuffed animal in the entire world. Who cared if bats kept the world safe for people who wished to enjoy the great nighttime outdoors? Who cared if this particular bat had been stuck inside a glass box for years on end, unable to fly, unable to eat even a single mosquito, let alone more than half its weight nightly in insects?

Julia Gillian put everything she had into her scowl.

Her eye and forehead muscles ached from the effort. This was a great scowl. This was perhaps the best scowl ever seen in the history of the world. She wished she could sidle over to the mirror to see just how magnificent it truly was, but that would ruin the effect.

"Poodle?" said Enzo.

"You don't get it."

"I get that you're angry. I get that you wanted the meerkat, but you got the bat."

"Not just that. Lots of things."

Enzo swung her legs over her indoor reading hammock and got up.

"I'm going to wash the dishes," she said. "You're welcome to join me in the kitchen if you get tired of scowling."

✿

Julia Gillian stood in Enzo's kitchen doorway and cleared her throat. Enzo was scrubbing a giant pot and singing a song that, as far as Julia Gillian could tell, had something to do with a whale. Enzo had a horrible singing voice, but she did not care. Enzo loved to sing and sing she would. Small rainbow-colored soap bubbles floated up out of the sink and drifted in the air of the galley kitchen. Enzo was a strong believer in soap.

Again Julia Gillian cleared her throat. Enzo appeared not to hear.

"AHEM," said Julia Gillian.

That was not a clearing of the throat. It was a word, loud and clear, not to be ignored: AHEM. Enzo glanced over.

"Care to dry?" she said.

Enzo hefted the enormous pot out of the sink and handed Julia Gillian a dish towel. Julia Gillian began to dry the pot. What else could she do? Enzo did not care about her unhappiness. It was possible that Enzo did not care about her at all.

"Did I ever tell you about the Dark Lady?" said Enzo.

Julia Gillian dried the enormous pot carefully. She made sure that every drop of water was gone by wiping the dish towel around and around, inspecting every square inch of pot surface. No pot in the history of the world had ever been dried with more care than this pot. If awards were given for pot drying, Julia Gillian would win one. She concentrated so intently on the pot that she did not answer Enzo for some time. Enzo kept washing dishes, stacking them in the rinse sink, and singing her tuneless song. Julia Gillian kept not answering, and Enzo kept singing.

"No," said Julia Gillian.

"No what?"

So much time had elapsed between Enzo's Dark Lady question and Julia Gillian's answer that Enzo had forgotten her own question.

"No, you never told me about the Dark Lady," said Julia Gillian.

"Oh yes, the Dark Lady."

Enzo finished washing the last glass and set it carefully on the rim of the drain sink. Now Julia Gillian, after spending so much time on the enormous pot,

faced a rinse sink full of soapy dishes waiting to be rinsed and dried. If Enzo did not insist on using so much soap, Julia Gillian's job would be easier. But that was the way it was in the world: Some people used too much soap, and others were forced to bear the consequences.

"Yes, the Dark Lady," said Enzo again.

She perched on the radiator. Julia Gillian focused on the sink of soapy dishes. She was listening to Enzo, but she was pretending not to listen.

"The Dark Lady hung on the other side of my closet door when I was little," said Enzo.

Julia Gillian rinsed a tall water glass carefully and dried it with equal care. Even if some people insisted on using too much soap, Julia Gillian was still going to do her job the right way.

"It didn't matter how tight I closed my closet door," said Enzo. "Every night, as soon as the light was out, there she was. The Dark Lady."

"Didn't you have a night light?"

Julia Gillian had not intended to say anything while Enzo was talking, but she just had.

"Sure, I had a night light," said Enzo. "But it didn't matter. Night came, and so did the Dark Lady."

"But if the closet door was shut tight, how did you know she was there?"

"I just knew."

As someone highly skilled in the Art of Knowing,

this made sense to Julia Gillian. She tried to picture what a Dark Lady might look like. Maybe a Dark Lady was similar to the Halloween masks at Bryant Hardware that had so scared the toddler twins.

"And you couldn't get rid of her?"

"No. She just hung there."

Julia Gillian considered this information. There were definite similarities between the Dark Lady and the green book. Both were scary, and both were unavoidable.

"When did she finally go away?" said Julia Gillian.

"Go away?" said Enzo. She sounded surprised. "She didn't. She's still there."

"The Dark Lady is still hanging on the other side of your closet door?"

"Yes."

"But aren't you scared?"

"No."

"Why not?"

"I just got used to her, Noodlie," said Enzo.

If the Dark Lady had never gone away, then Enzo must have gotten used to being afraid every night when she went to bed. This seemed like a bad situation to Julia Gillian, but Enzo sounded calm. Julia Gillian was going to have to think about this one.

"Here," said Enzo. "Let me help you dry."

And Enzo hopped down from the radiator and got another dish towel from the drawer below the silverware drawer, the better to help Julia Gillian.

CHAPTER TWENTY-TWO

A Mask of Their Own

Bigfoot was indeed entranced with the stuffed bat. Once inside the door of their apartment, he trotted in a businesslike manner straight to Julia Gillian's room, where he lay the bat on his long magenta pillow and gazed at it adoringly. Julia Gillian observed them for a minute, then she cleared her throat. Bigfoot did not even look up. She felt a bit jealous.

"That bat is nothing special, you know," she said to Bigfoot.

Bigfoot did not look up.

"Have you looked at it closely? It's nothing like the meerkat."

Bigfoot still did not look up. He stretched out, and

Julia Gillian could tell that he was about to doze off. The stuffed bat was next to him, held protectively under one paw. Julia Gillian frowned at the bat, which could not see her, of course.

"Bigfoot, do you love that bat more than you love me?"

No answer. Looking at Bigfoot and his bat, Julia Gillian felt lonely.

"Bigfoot," she whispered, hoping that her dog

would open his eyes, raise his head, ignore the bat, and thump his tail. "Bigfoot."

Nothing.

From the kitchen, Julia Gillian could hear the faint sounds of sloshing water and tearing paper. She also heard her parents, talking quietly, words and phrases drifting down the hall to Julia Gillian's ears.

How much flour do we add?

How long should the strips be?

What do we drape them over?

Boy, this is messy.

Given her powers of knowing, Julia Gillian knew immediately what her parents were up to. They were trying to make a mask of their own creation. Having no talent or experience with papier-mâché, they were nonetheless fumbling their way through the process. For a moment, Julia Gillian wanted to help them. *Just a little water,* she wanted to say, *and thin strips are better than thick. Try a balloon for draping.* But she kept still. This was her parents' job, and they needed to figure it out on their own. How else would they learn?

Julia Gillian sat on her bed and watched Bigfoot and the bat. Bigfoot and *his* bat, she silently corrected herself. In all honesty, it could not be said that the bat belonged in any way to her, so great was Bigfoot's devotion to the ratlike little thing. For years she had been trying to win the meerkat, but perhaps Bigfoot had secretly been longing for the bat.

"Did you want that bat all this time, Bigfoot?" said Julia Gillian.

No answer. Bigfoot and his bat were sound asleep. Down the hall, in the kitchen, the sounds of papier-mâché gradually stopped. Her parents must be finished with the mask of their own creation. *Good job, Mom and Dad,* beamed Julia Gillian telepathically.

The green book sat on the bookshelf. The ponytail holders were back around Julia Gillian's wrist. The ending was still in the green book, and it was still sad, but Julia Gillian had absorbed it into her heart already, so there was no need to try to hide it anymore. She crossed her legs and looked out her window, which was something that she could do, now that the quilt-pillow-whistling-marmot tower was gone. A soft breeze came wafting through the screen.

The kitchen was quiet. Whatever papier-mâché

creation that her parents had decided to make was made now. Frankly, Julia Gillian was a little apprehensive. What sort of papier-mâché creation would two grownups with no papier-mâché experience be able to produce? Julia Gillian feared for the quality of the mask. She felt a little sorry for her parents, who lacked her own talent.

She felt a little sorry for herself, too. No matter what she did, global warming, war, budget cuts, and the fact that she had won not her dream animal but a skinny brown bat would still be true. Julia Gillian thought about Enzo's Dark Lady, hanging on the other side of every closet door of Enzo's life.

Bigfoot suddenly raised his head and looked directly at Julia Gillian. He did this once in a great while. It was as if, while he was sleeping, Bigfoot were able to divine that Julia Gillian needed him, and he immediately woke and gazed at her, offering his help in his silent Bigfoot way. Julia Gillian smiled at him. Truly, he was the dog of her dreams.

"Tomorrow's Saturday, Bigfoot," she said. "Maybe Mom and Dad will take us to the Quang."

CHAPTER TWENTY-THREE

Being Afraid

The Quang Restaurant was at 28th and Nicollet, which meant that it was well outside the parameters of Julia Gillian's nine-square-block walk. Her parents were fans of walking, as was she, and it was their routine to walk to the Quang whenever possible.

"Neither snow nor rain nor heat nor gloom of night will keep us from the Quang," recited Julia Gillian to Bigfoot, who was still sleeping.

Julia Gillian was pretty sure that quote originally belonged to the post office, but it seemed appropriate tonight. It was still hot, even in the early evening, and while there seemed no chance of snow whatsoever, who knew what might happen, especially on the sort of discombobulated week that this one had turned out to be. Julia Gillian admired the bravery of this quote, and so she recited it again.

"Neither rain nor snow nor heat nor gloom of night," she said.

Bigfoot opened his eyes and thumped his tail twice.

"Daughter?" her father called from the living room.

"Father?"

"Might you be hankering for some egg rolls?"

This was her father's signal that he and her mother were ready to leave for the Quang.

"Indeed I might," called Julia Gillian.

"Excellent. And is there a dog somewhere in the vicinity who might be hankering for a stroll to Nicollet Avenue?"

"Indeed there is."

Now Bigfoot stretched and slowly pushed himself upright. He knew the Saturday night ritual as well as Julia Gillian. He shook his large head, yawned, and scooped up the stuffed bat in his jaws.

"Does that bat have to come with us?" said Julia Gillian.

But she already knew the answer.

On the way to the Quang, the Gillian family passed the redbrick house where the worried little girl lived. Would she be out? Thinking of how, only yesterday, the little girl had witnessed Julia Gillian flying down the sidewalk with Bigfoot obviously in control, she privately wished that the little girl would be safely inside her house.

But there she was, sitting on her steps, her shoes — still untied — beside her.

"Well, hello," said Julia Gillian's mother, who, as a first-grade teacher, naturally gravitated toward little children. "Are you excited about school?"

"No," said the little girl.

She gave Julia Gillian a significant look, a look that said, *You know my secret, but please don't tell it to these grownups.*

"Oh dear," said Julia Gillian's mother. "There's nothing to be afraid of, you know."

The little girl sighed. Julia Gillian could feel in her own self how tired the little girl was. She was tired of being afraid, and she was tired of grownups telling her that she had nothing to be afraid of. The fact of the matter, thought Julia Gillian, was that knowing you shouldn't be afraid was completely different from not being afraid. Julia Gillian thought of Enzo, and how when she was a little girl, Enzo had been afraid every single night.

Maybe there was no Dark Lady. Maybe the Dark Lady hanging behind Enzo's tightly closed closet door had actually been just a bathrobe, or even a shadow, but so what? Enzo had still been afraid.

"I just got used to it," Enzo had said.

Julia Gillian had been thinking about this for a while. Was just getting used to something that you couldn't do anything about another way of getting through it? Now, walking by the little girl and her untied shoes, Julia Gillian felt a surge of tenderness. She handed Bigfoot's leash to her father and squatted down beside the little girl. Bigfoot stood patiently, the bat flopped between his jaws. Julia Gillian's parents stopped walking and watched her with interest.

"This is private," said Julia Gillian, and she made a gentle shooing motion so that her parents would understand that she needed to speak to the little girl alone.

Bigfoot and Julia Gillian's parents ambled away down the sidewalk. The little girl sighed again. Julia Gillian knew from personal experience that it was not easy being an almost-kindergartener. It was beginning to seem as if every age had its particular difficulties.

"I know you're afraid," said Julia Gillian to the little girl.

She had not expected to say those exact words, but there they were.

"I know that everyone is telling you that you have nothing to be afraid of."

The little girl gazed off down the street, to where Julia Gillian's parents and Bigfoot were waiting at the end of the block. She was ignoring Julia Gillian, albeit in a polite way.

"And that the kindergarten teachers are so nice,

and they'll help you with your laces, and not to worry, and blah blah blah."

The little girl looked up, surprised. The *blah blah blah* had caught her attention.

"And they're right," said Julia Gillian. "But still. If you're afraid, you're afraid."

The little girl looked at Julia Gillian. She did not blink.

"And once in a while, whether they admit it or not, everyone is afraid," said Julia Gillian. "That's all I wanted to tell you."

The little girl looked at Julia Gillian some more, and after a while she nodded. Then she picked up her shoes, with their dangling laces, and walked up the steps and into her house.

CHAPTER TWENTY-FOUR

The Quang Restaurant

"Can I have a bubble tea?" said Julia Gillian. "A strawberry bubble tea, to be exact?"

"I don't know," said her father. "Can you?"

"*May* I have a strawberry bubble tea?"

"Yes. You may."

"You know, I think I'd like to try a bubble tea myself," said Julia Gillian's mother. "I'm feeling adventurous tonight."

Julia Gillian's mother reached up and adjusted the papier-mâché hat that she was now wearing. Her father was wearing one, too. Both the papier-mâché hats were lopsided and damp-looking, clearly the work of amateurs, but her parents kept glancing at her with hopeful expressions, waiting for her to say something about their misshapen headgear.

"You'll like your bubble tea, Mom," said Julia Gillian. "Strawberry's the best."

Julia Gillian's parents looked at each other. Her father adjusted his hat again. It kept listing sideways, and now he tilted his head to help the hat stay upright.

"Notice anything?" he said.

"Indeed I do," said Julia Gillian. "I notice that the Quang is crowded tonight. We were lucky to get the last booth."

"But do you notice anything else, honey?" said her mother, whose own hat kept slipping down and nearly covering her eyes, so that she was forced to tip her head up and look down her nose in order to see.

"Yes," said Julia Gillian. "Some people are better than others at making things out of papier-mâché."

"So you did notice!" said her father.

"Don't you want to take a closer look at our hats?" said her mother.

"Not right now," said Julia Gillian.

Her father with his tilting head and her mother with her barely visible eyes looked so disappointed that Julia Gillian relented a bit.

"Maybe later, though," she said. "Isn't it nice to have Bigfoot with us?"

The kind Quang people, who had known Julia Gillian and her family for years, had let Bigfoot come right into the restaurant tonight. He lay beneath the booth, out of sight despite his size.

"You've got to admit that bat is kind of cute," said Julia Gillian's father, nodding at the bat drooping out of Bigfoot's mouth.

"Meerkats are cute," said Julia Gillian.

"Still."

Julia Gillian peered under the tabletop and gave the bat a good look. He *was* kind of cute, in an unusual way, she supposed, with his over-large ears and his diminutive eyes. Maybe his eyes were not beady but, rather, frightened. *Bigfoot and I will take care of you*, she beamed telepathically to the bat. She reached down and stroked Bigfoot's ears.

Then she looked around the Quang. Here they were, she and her parents. The Quang was their favorite restaurant, and it made the best egg rolls in town, not to mention the bubble tea. Julia Gillian looked at the fat red Buddha in the corner altar. The Buddha held his belly and laughed. Sticks of incense were placed around him, and a mountain rose in the painted background behind him.

In the other corner of the Quang was the frozen treats freezer. In it were Popsicles of unusual flavors, such as lychee.

Then there was the counter, where the man in the yellow T-shirt and the girl with the extraordinarily long hair worked together, teasing and joking with the customers. Lined up before them were rows of plastic-wrapped slices of cassava cake and mochi balls in syrup.

If you wanted, you could order one to go when you paid for your dinner.

And here was the restaurant itself, filled with booths and green-topped tables and metal chairs with padded green seats. On each table was a container of chili oil, a bottle of soy sauce, and a holder filled with napkins and spoons and chopsticks. Julia Gillian was expert at using chopsticks. So was her mother. Her father still preferred a fork, but he was practicing. Before she started coming to the Quang, Julia Gillian had not been able to use chopsticks either.

She realized that she had mastered the art of chopsticks. Some time ago, in fact. Julia Gillian made a mental note that tonight, when she got home, she would heave the mattress up, extract her notebook, and add the Art of Chopsticks to the list.

And she had won at the claw machine. She had not won the animal of her dreams, but that did not change the fact that she was now a claw master.

She had also finished the green book. Did that mean that she was now a master of something else, something to do with certain books and their sad endings? Julia Gillian decided to think about that later. One accomplishment at a time was enough.

"Okay," said Julia Gillian. "I'll take a look at your hats now."

Her parents looked surprised, and pleased. They reached with relief to take off their hats, and they handed them to Julia Gillian. As she suspected, her parents had done an extremely poor job with their papier-mâché. These hats, if in fact they could be called hats, were lumpy, with globs of still-damp paste sticking out here and there. But they had tried, and that was what counted, wasn't it?

"What's the news today, Julia Gillian?" said her father.

"Yes, we're interested in knowing what's going on in the wider world," said her mother.

Julia Gillian took a closer look at the hats, and then she understood what her parents had done. They looked at her hopefully, waiting for her to read the words they had pasted on top of their lumpy headgear.

"Well," said Julia Gillian. "The weather report calls for 'hot sun but not too steamy, a perfect summer day in Minneapolis.'"

"Yes," said her father.

Julia Gillian turned the misshapen hat to the other side and read the words printed there.

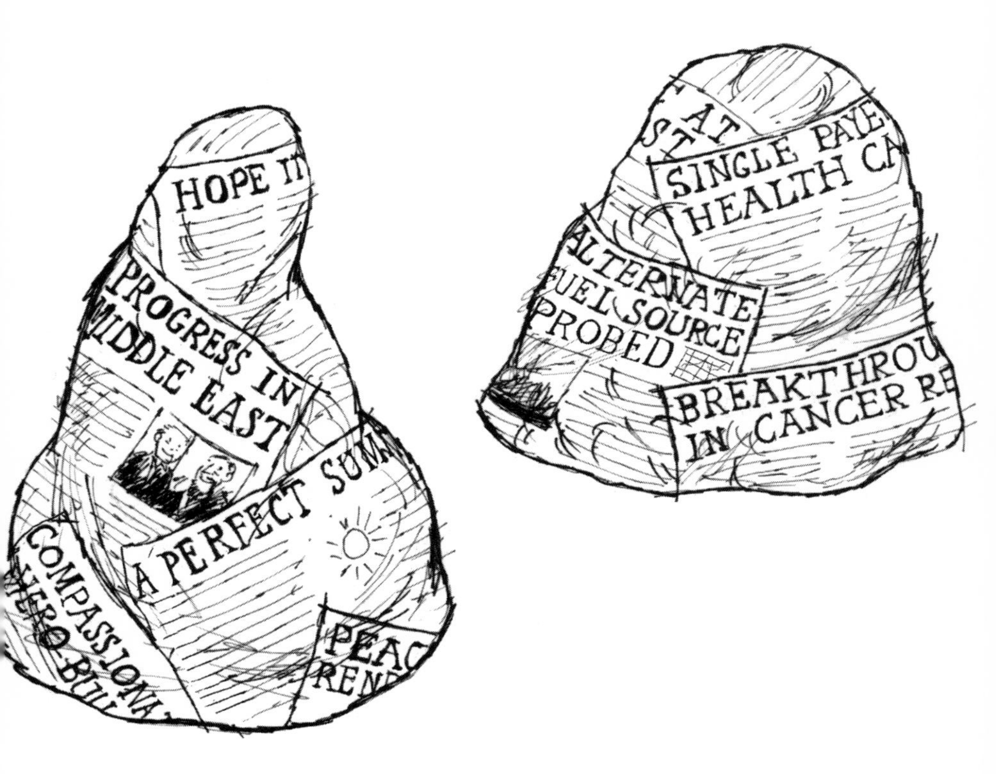

"'Progress in the Middle East,'" read Julia Gillian.

"Yes," said her mother.

"'Congratulations to ninety-four-year-old Bertha Whitman,'" read Julia Gillian, "'who just obtained her B.A. from Metropolitan State University.'"

She had no idea what a B.A. was, but she knew that it must be a good thing, because both her parents were smiling.

"That's good news," said Julia Gillian.

"We think so, too," said her father.

"We want to tell you something, Julia Gillian," said her mother.

"We want to tell you that we're sorry for spending so much time studying," said her father.

"And we promise to stay within better study parameters for the rest of the summer," said her mother.

"And we were wondering if you'd like to go to the water park tomorrow."

"And then have a picnic at the Rose Garden."

"Yes," said Julia Gillian. "Yes, yes, yes."

"Good," said her father.

"Good," said her mother. "We'll make cucumber sandwiches and bring the red-checked tablecloth."

Their waitress came over to the table. She was Julia Gillian's favorite waitress, the one with the beautiful smile.

"All finished?" she said. "I'll be back with the check."

When the waitress came back, she was carrying a bowl that she set down in the middle of the table. Three spoons poked out of it.

"Something for you," she said. "A Vietnamese dessert, on the house."

On the house meant "free." That meant that Julia Gillian and her parents were special and honored guests of the Quang. Julia Gillian looked into the bowl.

"Is that sweet rice?" she said. "And black-eyed peas? And coconut cream on top?"

The waitress nodded. Julia Gillian looked down at the dessert. It resembled something that Zap would experiment with in a recipe of his own creation. And at that exact moment, she looked up to see Zap and Enzo coming into the Quang. They were smiling in Julia Gillian's direction; they had seen her at the same time she had seen them. Julia Gillian waved.

"Look!" she said to her mother and father. "It's Zap and Enzo."

"So it is," said her mother.

"Zap!" called Julia Gillian. "I mastered the art of the claw!"

Zap gave her a double thumbs-up. Then he alternated both hands up and down in the air as if he were juggling, and he tilted his head at Julia Gillian the way Bigfoot did: *Are you ready to master the art of juggling?*

Julia Gillian nodded, and Zap gave her another thumbs-up. When you mastered one art, you could move on to another.

Julia Gillian turned back to the Vietnamese dessert.

"Should I try this?" she said.

"Definitely," said her father.

Julia Gillian dipped the spoon in and took a small bite. Sweet coconut and black-eyed peas and soft rice filled her mouth. It was perhaps the most delicious thing she had ever eaten. It was even more delicious than a strawberry bubble tea.

"Well?" said her mother.

"Well?" said her father.

Julia Gillian took another spoonful. All she could do was nod. This was as good as the tastiest of Zap's creations. It was as good as she had thought that winning the meerkat in the claw machine might be. It was as good as she had thought the green book would be, long ago when she first began reading it. She had not won the meerkat, and the green book did not have a happy ending. But here was this dessert. Who could have known that it would taste so good? The waitress came over and smiled and nodded.

"You like it?" she said.

"Indeed I do," said Julia Gillian.

This book was designed and art directed by Marijka Kostiw.
The jacket art and black and white interior illustrations were created digitally by Drazen Kozjan.
The display type was set in Mrs. Eaves Smart Lig, which is a font created in 1996
by Zuzana Licko, a font designer and cofounder of the Emigre type foundry.
Mrs. Eaves is based on the font Baskerville and named after Sarah Eaves, who became
Baskerville's wife and finished printing the volumes he left incomplete on his death.
The display was also set in F 2 F Madzine, a font designed in 1994 and 2003 by font designer
Alexander Branczyk, who is a partner of Frankfurt design company Xplicit.
The text type was set in 14-pt Adobe Garamond Pro, which was designed in 1989 by font designer
Robert Slimbach for Adobe, and is based on type designs of sixteenth-century printer Claude Garamond.
This book was printed at R. R. Donnelley & Sons Co. and production was supervised by Jess White.